Edited By: CaSondra Poulsen & Pamela Potter

Ocean's Edge

Ocean's Edge

Dedication

This book is dedicated to and inspired by my husband, the love of my life, who continues to inspire me to bring my creative thoughts and ideas out from where they are hidden deep within myself. I was like a glass half full, or empty, however you look at the glass. I was filled to an overflowing state when my husband walked into my life.

This book is also dedicated to all the generations that came before me; with love and respect for the sacrifices they made so that I could live in this great Nation with the freedoms and privilege that were made possible because of them. I say thank you.

My life, my love, my heart, my spirit, and my soul will always belong to one. Time, tide, wind, and waves have forever bound us together. Centuries will come and go, and we will be transformed into other bodies and have many names through to the end of time, but our spirits will forever be entwined—forever searching and seeking for each other.

Subtle hints from past lives always leave traces to remind us of each other—like beacons, leading us forever back to each other to live yet another life together.

Chapter One

It is a cold winter's night and I was fast
asleep, dreaming, when suddenly I awoke to
someone calling my name, over and over. I sit up
and looked around, but realize it was my dream. As
I lay my head back down onto the pillow, my
thoughts returned to the dream that was recurring,
night after night.

I live in a big, beautiful house that sits close
to the ocean's edge. I am always looking out the
window, watching the waves crashing against the
shore, when I am awakened by the voice of
someone calling me. When I wake again in the
morning, I realize I had fallen back to sleep,
thinking about the dream. I have been having it
every night now for weeks. In my waking hours, I

daydream about living in that house. I wonder how I will ever be able to explain the house well enough to have it built.

The phone rings and I reach for it. It's a dear friend of mine, Sean. After pleasantries, I explain to him about my dream house that I've seen every night for months.

"I would love to have it built someday."

He laughed. "It sounds just like Keith's house."

Yeah, sure it does, I thought, but said, "Isn't that the guy you've been trying to get me to go out with?"

"Same guy, Becca."

"So his name is Keith, is it?"

"Didn't I tell you his name before?"

"No, just a friend you have that I should meet up with sometime. You know, I've always liked that name, Keith. When I was a little girl I even wanted to grow up and marry someone named Keith," I said, rubbing the sleep from my eyes.

He laughed. "So what happened to that dream?"

"Funny, Sean," I said. "You're just full of humor, aren't you?"

"Why, here's your chance to find your dream man named Keith."

"Again with the humor," I said dryly. "I think I will stay alone the rest of my life. I feel it's better for me to spend my life alone than to be with the wrong guy again."

"Ok, got it. You don't want me to fix you up with anyone." Then he asked, "What are your plans for New Year's Eve?"

"I don't have any. I'll just have a quiet night at home and go to bed early."

"You can't spend it alone! You have to go and do something!"

"Sean," I interrupted, "I don't have to go anywhere, or be with others, to make me any happier or fulfilled. I am fine spending it alone."

"I don't want you to be alone. It would bother me." He admitted. "Would you please consider going out with me and some friends? We're all going together to a local Bar &Grill and we're having a private party. I would love for you to come. You'd have a great time and you already know several of the people. It would give you time to catch up with them and listen to a good band we've gotten to play for us."

"Let me think about it and I'll get back with you." I tried to put him off, but he persisted.

"I have to know so I can reserve you a spot."

I gave in. "Well all right, I guess, but no trying to fix me up!" I admonished.

"Ok. I promise I won't do that to you on New Year's Eve. We're meeting about 8:30 at Salty's in Southport. You know where that's at, don't you?"

"I think so, but I'll look up the address just to make sure."

"Well, now that we have that settled, what else is going on with you?" He sounded pleased to have lured me out.

"To be honest Sean, I have to confess, I have a restless spirit as of late, and I just can't put my finger on what's causing it. I feel like something life changing is going to happen any minute."

"Life changing, huh? You don't sound worried."

"I'm not worried, just restless."

"Well, if you aren't worried about it then I won't either. Call me if you need anything, or if you just want to talk between now and New Year's Eve." He said as we hung up the phone.

I hadn't told anyone about my spirit feeling restless, and certainly not about my feeling that something was about to happen to change my whole life. In my head it hadn't seemed strange, but now that I'd said it out loud, well, life changing, that's big. I wondered what in the world would, or could, be so life changing. I couldn't wrap my head around it, so I busied myself.

I grabbed my oil paints and a canvas and brought my easel into the living room. I had a vision in my head of what I thought the old man in the sea looked like. His eyes, lost in great thought, as if he were casting out his thoughts for the pounding waves to carry them off to his love on a faraway shore, like an ocean-tossed love letter in a bottle. Since I was a young girl, he has been everything I envisioned an old salty sea captain to look like, I decide with satisfaction. As I finished the last stroke of paint and signed my name I felt a strange connection to the sea captain, as if he was alive and had a gentle soul. I could feel his thoughts were as deep as the sea, like the captain had a story to tell, deeper and more meaningful than most. I knew as I signed the painting I would never part with it. Eventually, I would hang it on the wall of the house of my dreams.

The day passed without notice. I'd been absorbed in painting and night had fallen by the time I left the painting on the easel to dry. After a shower and a quick meal, I picked up a book and thought about my comfy chair, but I was already sleepy so I got right into bed. I didn't make it two pages before I fell into a deep sleep. I'd grown accustom to this routine of being awaken by the same dream night after night, so when I woke to the same voice calling my name, I went back to sleep without another thought. I soon found I was caught up in my dream but this time no one was calling my name. Tonight I was sitting in a chair facing a large glass window. As I looked out onto the ocean's waves gently coming ashore, I felt home again, such a feeling of peace within my soul that it was difficult to describe.

Every sense within my body was at peace all at one time. No cares. No worries. Nowhere had I to be but there. I wasn't alone. My spirit was filled with the love of another. I was complete and whole with no thought of anything but the love of another spirit surrounding me with its gentle kindness.

As I woke, the loving spirit was still with me. Then, it was gone. I crawled out of bed and walked into the living room. I had forgotten about painting the salty sea captain the day before. His eyes were the first thing I saw as I entered the room. I stopped and looked at him, wishing I had a wall large enough to hang him on now. One day soon, I thought as I walked into the kitchen to make a pot of coffee.

The coffee brewed, and I got dressed and took another easel out of the back room. I set it up in the living room with a fresh canvas. As I went back into the kitchen to pour a much needed cup of coffee, I gazed out the kitchen window. The ground was covered in snow, and the clouds looked as if they were about ready to flood the earth with more. It didn't take me long to decide what I wanted to paint on the new canvas. Spring flowers, to rush winter out and welcome spring in. If only it was that easy. I painted flowers in bloom for days, all colors and kinds. Each night I was awaken by the voice calling my name and fell back to sleep as fast as I woke.

Chapter Two

A week had come and gone since I had talked to Sean. It would be nice to get out of the house and surround myself with old friends. Maybe that was why my soul was growing more restless each day. I needed to get out. I had been in the house by myself going on a week and a half and had only talked to Sean and a couple family members in that time. I thought most people must have been indoors with few trips out given all the snow we'd had of late. But tonight the roads looked clear and the weatherman predicted no snow, so a change of view would be nice. I will paint till around six, I told myself, and then get dressed for my big night out with friends. The day went by quick and as I readied to go out, my spirit jumped with excitement. I couldn't imagine why I was so excited just to see old friends.

Dressed and ready, I made my way to the car. The closer I got, the more exited I felt within my soul. I had never felt this way before. It felt crazy! I was sure I would calm down once I met up with everyone. I decided to call Sean before I went in to see if he was already there or what time he would arrive. His phone rang a few times before he finally answered.

"Hi, Sean, you inside Salty's?"

"Oh, Becca!" he cried, "I meant to call you! My girlfriend changed our plans at the last minute. We're going to her boss's house. I am so sorry."

I was startled. "I guess I'll just go home. I haven't gone in yet."

"No! Absolutely not," he said. "Craig and Sue, and Kevin and Marlo are all wanting to see you, along with some other friends you haven't seen in a while. Promise me you'll go in and a least say hello."

"Ok," I sighed. "I will, but I'm not staying long though."

"Ok. Just go in 'til you're ready to go home."

"You talked me into it. I'm going. I'll call you tomorrow."

I sat in the car a few minutes and wondered if I really wanted to go in without Sean and Debbie. After a few moments, I openend the car door. Crossing the parking lot, I paused when I reached for the door knob. As my hand touched the door, I thought my spirit was going to explode with unexpected excitement that turned to peace as I finally opened the door. I suddenly felt as if my spirit was connected to another spirit—a good, peaceful soul. I thought, what in the world is going on with me? As I made my way into Salty's Bar and Grill, I quickly looked around to find familiar faces, feeling uncomfortable and out of place by myself. I soon found Lisa and went straight to her. She and Mike greeted me with a big hug, and then Frank and Beth did, too. It felt nice to be among friends for the evening, but I kept scanning the whole place, looking for someone specific as I sat down.

I looked across the table and my eyes met the one my soul had been searching for. I knew it instantly. No words had been spoken. I had never seen this man before. But even as I sat there, I knew I would spend the rest of my life with him. My mind whirled at such a thought, as if trying to keep up with what my spirit felt. What in the world is going on? I asked myself. How could I even tell this was the man I would spend the rest of my life with? I wasn't looking for anyone to be with or love. I was fine without anyone in my life, yet a man I had never met was sitting across the table from me and suddenly he was going to be the man I would spend the rest of my life with. I didn't know his name. I'd never heard his voice. I didn't even know if he was married or not. What was I doing? Even as my brain scrambled to catch up, my whole being and everything within me decided he was my soulmate and the man I would be with the rest of my life.

I hadn't even stopped to look at the man himself. I only saw his spirit shining through his blues eyes.

I stared for a moment and then Frank started to talk to me.

"It's been awhile since Ginger and I have seen you. Where you been hiding?"

"Inside, out of the cold and snow."

"That sounds like the best place to me," Wayne said, then asked, "So, are you dating anyone?"

"No," I answered. "I just find being by myself works best for me."

"Been awhile since you dated, hasn't it?"

"It has, but you know, it's been by choice, not because of a lack of offers."

"Well, I knew that it wasn't from the lack of offers," Wayne said, then changed the subject. "So, do you know everyone at the table?"

Before I could answer, a voice came across the table and said, "No, I haven't met your friend."

That voice. Where had I heard it before? It was as if I had known the sound of that voice for a long time. Then it hit me—my dream—the voice that called my name every night, looking for me in my dream house. What I am I going to do now? I asked myself. Before Wayne could even say another word, the voice from across the table stood up and reached out his hand.

"Hello, I'm Keith."

It was in that moment I paused to look at the man behind the blue eyes and warm comforting spirit. I guessed him to be six foot one with a strong build, dark brown hair, and a great smile.

Keith. Of course, his name would be Keith, I thought. I extended my hand. "I'm Becca."

As our hands connected our eyes met. I shook quickly and let his hand go, afraid if I held it too long I wouldn't be able to let go. Surely the woman sitting next to him must be his wife. My brain was ready to explode with so many conflicting emotions. I forced myself to calm down and take it one step at a time. I took three deep breaths then I smiled and asked, "Is that your wife?"

"This is Sandy," Keith said as I extended my arm politely to shake hands, certain this was the end of my flight of fantasy. "But she's not my wife. I'm not married."

I gave Sandy a pleasant greeting. Just because they weren't married didn't mean they weren't together. I was still processing all this when he asked, "How long have you known this crowd?"

"Oh, going on five years now. How long have you known them?"

"The same, many years. I am surprised we never met before."

"Do you know Sean, too?" I asked.

"I do." Keith answered. "I've known Sean going on seven years. Matter of fact, I thought he was coming tonight."

"He was, but he and his girlfriend got invited last minute to her boss's house, so they went there."

This must be the Keith Sean was talking to me about. He told me Keith was single and lived by himself. The guy Sean had been trying to fix me up with and I kept telling him, no. I wondered if that was old news and he'd found a girlfriend.

The band they hired finally finished setting up and started to play. Everyone got up to dance, leaving me alone at the table. Keith had asked Sandy to dance, so there must be something going on. *What I am going to do now? I've seen him and felt his spirit and heard his voice. I have committed*

my whole being to him already. And there he is on

the dance floor with Sandy. I want to cry.

The song ended and everyone returned to the table, but as fast as they sit down the band starts playing another song, this time a slow one. Before I could think about it, everyone is getting up again. I looked across the table at Sandy, still sitting alone. I thought he must have gone to the restroom or something when I heard his voice behind me.

"Would you like to dance?" I turned to see him holding out his hand. I wasn't sure what to say, but he asked again, "Please, do me the honor of dancing with me."

I put my hand in his and headed for the dance floor. He turned me to face him and put his arms around my back, pulling me close. I felt as if I was born to be nowhere but in his arms.

My mind raced to the end of the night. *What happens when it's time to go home? How will I ever be able to leave this man and go home without him? How can I even think this way? I have never felt this way before about any man, let alone one I just met.* The song ended and Keith took my hand to walk me back to my seat.

When the band started playing "Mustang Sally" Lisa said, "Come on, Becca, let's dance!"

I quickly got up and headed to the dance floor with her. Marlo joined us and we're all dancing together when Mike and Frank join us. Before I knew, it Keith and Sandy were also on the dance floor as the band went straight into " Mony

Mony" We were all dancing together. As the band finished up the song, they led right into a slow song. The couples were moving toward each other, into each other's arms.

I was retreating to the table when I heard Keith asking, "Becca, come dance with me." I turned and went straight into his open arms. As he drew me close into him, I looked up into his eyes. No words had to be spoken. Everything we had to say to each other was being spoken through our spirits, deep within. I knew our souls were forever connected, as if they had known each other for centuries. When the song ended I don't know, but we kept dancing, Keith holding me ever so closely in his arms, my head on his chest.

Wayne broke in. "Hey you two! Get with the beat!"

We slowly moved apart, Keith sliding his hand in mine and walking me to my seat. Before Keith could get to his seat Sandy met him half way and asked him to dance with her again. I couldn't figure out their relationship. Surely if it was serious he'd be dancing the love songs with her, not me. Maybe it was a slow ending of a relationship? Just two friends out for New Year's Eve so they wouldn't be alone? We've all gone out at some time or another with an old friend to just catch up and have fun. My mind raced in all directions for an explanation.

The night drew to a close. The lead singer announced, "This is the last dance of the year and of the century. Let's rock in the new and out the old. Everyone come dance!"

We were all on the dance floor when the band stopped midway to count down the last ten seconds of the year. When they got to one, everyone started blowing horns and throwing confetti and hugging and kissing. That is when I headed back to my seat. I made my way from hug to hug as we all wished each other a Happy New Year. I almost made it off the dance floor when suddenly, there was Keith standing in front of me. He looked me in the eyes and kissed me on the lips.

"Happy New Year," he said.

I was returning the wish when Craig came up and hugged me. As Keith shook Craig's hand, I made my way back to my seat. I sat there, thinking.

The night was ending. It was time to leave and make my way home. How was I going to find the strength to leave this place and Keith? I watched my friends say their goodnights and head for the door. I can't stay later than Keith, I thought. It won't look good. So I picked up my coat and purse and slowly forced myself out of my seat. I said my goodbyes to friends and looked Keith in the eyes one last time.

"Goodbye, it was nice meeting you," I said, and I turned to walk out the door. I kept telling myself that I would see him again as I forced myself out the door. I started crying. The bond was there. It was true. And I believed it, but that didn't make the drive home any easier.

A few long days went by as I waited for a call from Keith. I never gave him my phone number, but I knew he would call. I had no doubt. The question was, how long would it be before he did? Three days after meeting him, he finally called. My heart leapt when the phone rang. I knew it was Keith on the other end when I answered, and that the questions I had would be answered before our eyes would meet again.

"Hi, this is Keith. I was wondering if you would like to go to lunch tomorrow."

"I would love to," I said, without hesitation.

"What is your address?"

"4352 Oceanview Drive. Do you know where that is?"

"I do. It won't be any trouble to find. Is noon okay?"

"Yes. Noon is perfect. But, what about Sandy? I don't want to get in the middle of someone else's relationship."

"Sandy and I are not in a relationship. We dated off and on for a few years, but I only felt friendship toward her. She wanted more and we both moved on. We were at the party together because I purchased the tickets months ago. It was more obligatory than an effort to rekindle things."

"Oh," I said, my heart racing.

"I had to go to Beth and Frank to get your number. Somehow they were not surprised. They said everyone at Salty's could see the love-light beaming from our eyes as soon as we met and it just grew brighter as the evening went on. They said they would have been shocked if I hadn't asked for your number." He paused and then said, "Does that seem strange to you?"

"Maybe it should, but no, not at all." My heart was full of joy as I hung up.

The day dragged into evening in anticipation of lunch with Keith the next day. I went to bed early with the book I was reading, *Chasing America's History*. Reading helped to occupy my mind so I was able to sleep. It didn't take as long as I feared before I fell asleep. As had become usual, I woke to a voice calling my name in the house of my dreams. But this time when I woke, I knew deep within my soul who the voice belonged to. It was the man I knew I would spend the rest of my life with—it was Keith's voice. I was comforted.

Chapter Three

I was ready when Keith got to my home the next afternoon, anxious, but trying not to show it. He drove to a restaurant close to the house, one we had both visited many times, just never together. We stayed until the servers were setting up for dinner, talking. We didn't even notice the time until the waitress came to ask us if we were staying for dinner, too. We chose to leave and left her a big tip. Keith told me as we made our way to the car that he had promised to go to his brother Sam's house and help him out with a project he had been working on. Keith drove me home and we said our goodbyes at the door. He asked if I was busy the next day. He wanted to take me to a restaurant close to his house that he thought I would enjoy. I told him I would love to go out to lunch with him again tomorrow.

"Can I call later this evening when I get home from his brother's? I would enjoy talking with you some more tonight," he said.

"Sure, I would love to talk to you later tonight."

We both lingered on my front porch, not wanting to part from each other, but I knew his brother Sam was waiting on him and if I invited him in he wouldn't make it to his brother's house.

"I guess I better let you go so you can help your brother. I don't want to be the reason you're late."

"I wouldn't go if I hadn't already promised him."

"That's fine," I said. "I'll talk to you later." I watched him drive away before going inside.

I never expected to be in this position in my life. My heart, soul, and body wanted to never part from him. My mind was way behind, still wondering exactly what was going on. I knew once any part of our flesh touched again our whole lives would change forever. We would be forever together, through the rest of our walk through life. I knew in my heart it was just a matter of time, but my mind was having trouble processing it. As I pondered how we would transition our lives into one, the phone rang. It is Keith.

"I finished and I'm back home."

"So, where do you live?"

"St. Gen, do you know where that is? Have you ever been here?" he asked.

"I've been there and I love it!" St. Gen was a quaint small town steeped in history. "Is that where we will be having lunch tomorrow? Where?" I asked, excited.

"A restaurant called, The Brick, have you been there before?"

"I haven't."

"I thought after we ate we could walk around town and go in some of the shops if it's a nice out."

"That sounds lovely. I look forward to spending the day with you."

"Me, too, Becca. Tomorrow can't get here soon enough for me."

It was late and although neither of us wanted to, we hung up the phone to get a good night's sleep. I showered, picked up the book on my night stand and climbed into bed. Before I opened the book, I let my mind wonder to Keith and the pure love I had for him. I was so amazed how he was a part of my dreams. Before I even met him, he was calling out to me. For over a month, every night he was in my dreams, and now the voice calling me was a part of my life forever. I opened *Chasing America's History* and started to read but my eyes were too heavy. I put the book back on the nightstand as I rolled over and fell asleep. I woke to Keith's voice searching for me. We found each other in the living room of my dream house and he drew me into his arms. Go back to sleep, I thought, you'll see him tomorrow.

Chapter Four

Morning came and woke me with the sun shining through my window. Today, I jumped to my feet, like a child on Christmas morning. I went to the kitchen and started a pot of coffee and then went straight to the bathroom to brush my hair and teeth and dress for the day. I changed ten times before I decided on what to wear. I loved that I was tall, 5'8 with long legs. I was pretty comfortable with my whole body, being around 130 to 135 in weight, hazel eyes and long, reddish-brown wavy hair. I was glad I had a couple hours to get ready before Keith got there. I never had a problem catching or keeping a man's attention. I used to try and play down my looks. But now was different. Of course, I wanted Keith to love me for my inner self and the person I am, but I also wanted him to be physically attracted to me, also. Now, dressed and full of a couple cups of coffee for breakfast, a knock came at the door.

"Good morning," he said with a big smile.

"Good morning. Come on in while I get my purse and put on my coat. How is the weather outside today?"

"Beautiful and sunny! It should be great for walking around Ste.Gen."

"Great, well, I am ready to go if you are."

"I am," he says with a smile. "Let's go and get the day started."

When we got to his car he opened the door for me and closed it carefully. As he got into the driver's seat, he slowly reached over and took my hand into his. He caressed my hand the whole way to the restaurant. When we arrived, he quickly got out of the car and opened my door, holding his hand out for mine. As we reached the restaurant door he extended his arm to open it. We were seated right away and ordered immediately. We sat again for hours, talking after we ate, as we had the day before. When the waitress came and asked if we needed anything else we decided it would be a great time to go out and walk around town. As we made our way out of the restaurant, Keith put my hand into his. It already seemed natural for my hand to be in his. We walked and went into all the quaint shops in town and took advantage of the beautiful sunny, warm January day. I hadn't even stopped to think until that moment that it was a new century and we welcomed it in together as I squeezed his hand ever so slightly. We had been walking in and out of little shops all day, all offering something a little different than the one before, but the one I loved the most was By The Boardwalk. They carried wooden rustic looking handmade bowls and leather journals that were hand-stitched and the paper was watermarked with an old Galeon ship. We spent hours going in and out of all the shops as the sun was starting to set behind the clouds. A chill started to fill the air.

"Becca would you like to see where I live? It's only about ten minutes from here."

"Sure, I would love to." We got into his car and drove to his house, my hand in its new favorite place, held in his. As we got closer to his house, he told me there was a long driveway and his house was the last house down the drive. When we came to a peak in the drive, he pointed. "That's my house there."

"Stop! Please, stop!" I said.

"What's the matter, Becca? Why do you want me to stop?" His voice filled with panic. "Don't you want to go to my house?"

"Keith, can I tell you a couple things before we go any further?"

"Sure, what is it?" he asked as he put the car into park.

"Hear me out. You might think I'm crazy and turn around and take me home, so I better tell you before we get all the way down the hill to your house." I took a deep breath. "I've been dreaming of your house every night for months. I wake up every night hearing your voice calling to me, even before we actually met. I can tell you exactly what your house looks like before we even go inside. I want to describe it so you can tell me if I am right before I go inside, that is, if you still want me to come."

I described every inch of the inside as he looked into my eyes and listen to every word I spoke. "My soul had been feeling restless for months leading up to our first meeting. The night we met, the closer I got to Salty's the more my spirit jumped with excitement and joy. When I grabbed the door knob and opened the door, I felt your spirit connecting to mine, as if they had been tied as one in another lifetime and were reconnecting after a long absence. I feel we have met in another lifetime, Keith."

Keith looked at me with his eyes wide open in amazement and hung onto every word until I finished. "Becca, you have completely described my whole house. You didn't leave out anything. As soon as I looked into your eyes, I knew I had to make you a part of my life. No, I don't think you're crazy, and yes, I still want you to come into my house and see the house of your dreams." Keith put the car back into drive and we made our way down the hill. Pulling into the garage, he quickly got out and came around to open my door. As he opened the door to his home, he said, "Here is the home of your dreams, Becca, I hope you like it as much in person as in your dreams."

I slowly walked in with Keith's hand in mine. I wanted to fall to the floor in disbelief when he pulled me into his arms and asked me what I thought. I stood for a few moments trying to take in everything. The house was everything I had dreamed of. The large glass window that was as long and tall as a wall would be. The fireplace in the center of the living room made of stone he had gotten from an old, stone house that had been torn down. The kitchen with an 11x8 slab of white granite with the natural cuts from the quarry it came from. It was primitive looking and beautiful at the same time. All the furniture was placed exactly where it was in my dream. From the leather couch to the winged back chairs. To the kitchen table that was made of oak that was long, wide and undeveloped in look.

"Becca, come sit on the couch as I light a fire and we can sit and talk about where we go from here. I know we just met, but I want you to move in with me and see where this journey leads us."

"I don't know, Keith. I want nothing more than to be with you, but I had already decided to spend the rest of my life alone."

"I had, too, so I know this is a big step for the both of us. But what else can we do? Neither of us wants to be away from each other. We feel drawn to each other beyond our control. I don't want to ever have to take you home or be without you. As a matter of fact, I was hoping you would stay the weekend with me and then Monday we'll go get your things and bring them here. I figure you could use one of my shirts to sleep in, and I have an extra toothbrush I bought just in case I could convince you to stay. If you want you can sleep in the guest bedroom. I just don't want you to leave me. I want to make this *our* house. Let's just play it by ear for a couple hours and see what transpires naturally."

As he finished lighting the fire, he sat beside me on the couch and pulled me close. He turned to look me in the eyes, then leaned closer until our lips met in a passionate kiss. I don't know if it was one long kiss or many with barely a breath in between. With one arm around my waist and the other hand holding mine, we kissed and kissed and every thought left me. Our spirits and bodies were connecting and the moment grew from simple kissing into love and passion.

For a moment I worried that our bodies wouldn't be as perfectly matched as our souls, so I decided that nature would rule the night to find out if we could match physically with the fire that already existed between our souls. As Keith kissed me, I drew my hand away from his and laid it on his leg, rubbing gently. His now free hand made its way to my breast, then moved upj to unbutton my top. Our passionate kiss broke as his warm lips moved down to my bare breast and my hand drifted up his inner thigh. His hands made their way to the hem of my skirt, then drifted under to slide up my thighs. The next thing I knew we were undressing each other, ever so slowing and gently, as the fire in the fireplace roared with flames and the wood crackled.

Night had completely fallen and the only light was from the fire. In moments we were standing naked, looking, touching each other when Keith took me into his arms and laid me on the couch.

He enter into me with his body as if he knew every part and how to touch me, the way two lovers that have made love over and over understood and knew automatically. He kissed my lips. As our bodies entwined, our souls further connected. We exploded with pleasure at the same time, as Keith pulled me as close as two separate bodies could be.

I screamed out my pleasure and he whispered in my ear, "I love you, Becca."

"And I you, Keith."

We stayed tightly connected, neither of us wanting to let go of the moment. We stayed the night there before the fire. We made love four times before the morning light finally convinced us to untwine our bodies. We showered and dressed together, and then went into the kitchen and made coffee.

Gazing into each other's eyes Keith said, "Becca, I love you and want to spend the rest of my life with you."

"And I you, Keith."

"I want to go get your things and move you into our home so we can start our lives together, unless you would rather us live in your house."

I looked at him. "I'd rather live here, Keith, but I have to tell you, I'm pretty independent and have lived by myself for a long time now."

He smiled. "Good, I'm glad you're independent. I have no desire to control you or keep you from your dreams. I just want to be part of it. I'm independent, too. I want you to share that and be the best part of my life. Do you think we are moving too fast? Do you think it is possible just to date and see each other only on the weekends? I don't. I can't imagine us being and living apart."

"I just never thought if I fell in love that it would ever be like this."

"What's bothering you?"

"Nothing, it's just hard for my mind to grasp. I can't quite get my head around us and this house. It's not every day a woman literally has her dream man and dream house all come to life in a moment. Keith, I can't imagine my life without you now that we found each other."

"Becca, I know you have been with other men and I have been with other women. We've both been married and divorced. What I found in you and with you comes once in a lifetime, and never for some people." I knew that he truly felt as I did.

"I know the difference between love and lust, and passion and desire," I said. "I know how often couples love unequally. What we have is true and real at every level. I can't, and won't, do anything to separate us from each other. So, after we eat we can go get my things because I can't sleep anywhere ever again without your arms around me and our bodies as entwined as our spirits."

"I could not have said it better myself. I've never been so lost for words to describe how I feel for anyone before, but I've never felt like this before either. And I never will again. I never believed in soulmates before, but I do now. There is no other way to describe my feelings and love than that. That each breath you take in and out is a moment more of life I have with you. How wonderful life will be having you to share it with."

I shuffled my feet, looking into my coffee. "Keith, I do need to go to my mom's this morning. Each of us kids go once a month and today is my day to see her. Would you like to go with me?" I looked up at his gentle eyes and continued, "She knows I had a date with you yesterday. She'll worry if I don't come to see her."

He chuckled. It was a warm sound. "Do you plan to tell her we are going to move in together?"

"I know she'll ask me when I plan to see you again, so I will do my best to explain everything for her. She'll think I'm nuts." I took a sip of coffee as I continued to watch him over the rim and through the steam swirling around my nose.

In my head, I tried to play the conversation I would have with my mom before I called her to assure her I was fine and that everything was good and the path I was taking was right for me.

The phone rang several times before she picked up. I checked to see how her day was going before I asked if she'd mind if Keith and I came by later. I knew that would put her at ease and I could introduce them before she had the chance to ask all her questions. She told me that would be great and that she and Jeff, my stepfather, looked forward to us coming by. I hung up the phone and Keith and I headed out.

"Are you anything like your mother?" he asked on our way out the door.

"Only in a few areas."

Keith continued to ask all the usual questions so I told him about my parents and family as we drove to their house. I thought Keith might get a little nervous meeting them, but as we got out of the car and made our way to the front door, he confessed to me he was excited. That put me more at ease. I thought how wonderful life was now that I'd met the man I could spend the rest of my life with, someone who would share my path without reservation or doubt.

I knocked on the door as I opened it, calling out to Mom. We exchanged all the usual greetings as she encouraged us to come in quickly and not let the cold in. We refused an offer of coffee and Jeff took our coats as we all sat down. I introduced Keith. We must have talked an hour before Mom offered coffee again. This time we accepted and as mom and I were making our way to the kitchen, Keith and Jeff were talking about mom and John's home. Jeff was telling Keith that the house was built in the 30's era, but they did a lot of remolding. He told Keith how he had opened up the ceiling in the living room to make it project to the mind's eye bigger and spacer then it really was. The kitchen door had barely shut behind us before Mom was talking about Keith.

"Well, Becca, I see you have met your soulmate."

I was so surprised I nearly dropped the serving tray I was setting up. I had never heard my mother utter any such thing.

"What did you say?" I asked.

"I see you met your soulmate," she repeated.

"Mother," I said, "I never heard you so much as mention soulmates before."

"Well, you never met yours before."

"Mom, remember that recurring dream I've been having every night for over a month now?"

"Yes."

"Remember that voice I kept hearing call my name? And the house I was seeing?"

"Yes, what about it?"

"It was Keith's voice I was hearing. And it's his house I was seeing."

"Becca, I could tell right away he was the man for you, and you the woman for him. The love-light shines bright from down deep within both of your souls."

It was still shocking to hear this from my mother. "I never, ever heard you talk like that to anyone, ever."

"There was no reason to before. I haven't talked to any of you kids like this 'til now. Thought I never would. Most people don't meet their soulmates. They're few and far between, but when two people do, everyone can see it just watching them together."

There would never be a better time, so I tossed out, "I'm moving in with Keith. When we leave here we're going to my house to pack my things."

Mother just looked at me. "I already figured it was something like that when you called and wanted to come by. Becca, if you thought you were going to shock me, you didn't. Seeing both of you together, I would've been more shocked if you didn't tell me you were. And here's another shock for you. Not only am I certain you two are soulmates, your Keith fits into the family as if he's been a part of it for a long time."

"So you like him?"

"Becca, I already truly care for him and think of him as part of the family."

"We better get back to living room with the coffee before they come looking for us." That was all very enlightening, although I wasn't sure exactly who was enlightened.

We walked into the living room and my eyes gravitated straight to Keith's eyes. I handed him and Jeff their coffee. Mother had hers, so I grabbed a cup for myself as I sat down by Keith's side. We talked a half an hour more, then announced we were going to head out. The day was getting away from us and we need to get some packing done.

Keith and I headed toward my house. As we drove, we decided to spend the night at my house and get as much packed as we could. The next morning, we would rent a U-Haul and then close the house up for the winter. In the spring, we'd get the rest and put the house on the market. We stopped at the U-Haul place on the way and arranged for Keith to pick up the truck the next morning. We'd make two trips. He'd drive the truck and I'd drive his car, then mine. When we got to my house we started packing things up right away. It felt so right to work next to him, even though we'd only just met in this life.

We had been hard at it for hours when we stopped to make something to eat. We found ourselves drawing closer, our hands tightening, then our lips met and we embraced. One minute we were in the kitchen, the next we'd moved to the bedroom. The next thing I knew, our bodies were entwined together as they had been the night before, fused together as we shared our love for each other. We made love into the late hours of the night. When morning came, neither of us wanted to separate our bodies to do anything. Keith wished me a good morning and offered me a kiss. I was happy to give one back and instead of jumping out of bed to get the early start we'd planned, his arms drew me closer, his lips made their way back to my breast and passion seemed like a much better start to the day. We took our time and when our bodies exploded with our passion, we were completely fulfilled, knowing we belonged to each other. After a while, we slowly separated and made our way out of bed and down the hall to the shower, building caresses into our showering.

Eventually, we turned to more practical activities. We dressed and ate breakfast, then we started our day. We made good time getting me moved. Two truckloads and then we were together in our home, as we would be forever. Everything seemed to flow with ease for both of us. We got everything placed where we wanted it. Clothes were unloaded and put away. Even the picture I painted of the old man in the sea was hanging over the fire place, just where I had envisioned it hanging. I felt home.

The dreams of the house and Keith calling my name out stopped. I had a dream three days after I moved in but it was new. There was a perfect circle with a bright light shining through the circle, then a voice came from within the bright light saying, "You and Keith are the perfect circle and I am the light shining through and in you, reuniting your souls."

I wasn't looking for or seeking confirmation, but received it gratefully as a gift. I have never doubted the love or the joining of our souls together since I opened the door at Salty's. It was like a door, a beginning, to the next chapter of my life on earth. Everything before was just preparation leading up to me being in tune to myself, so I would be able to recognize and sense and know what was real and before me.

Chapter Five

Keith and I married soon after moving in together. The days, months, and years seemed to fly by for us. Oh, of course, like everyone else in the world we had our ups and downs, but our love never wavered and our bond grew and grew. I realized the longer we were together the more my senses seemed to be enlightened, and the more focused I become of my awareness.

When I first met Keith I had halfheartedly told him I thought we'd met in another life. But as the years went by I felt more and more certain of it. I was doing research for my mother on our family tree. My grandmother had started the project but didn't get it finished. My mother really wanted to finish tracking down the proof that our family came over on the *Mayflower*. My Aunt Mary and brother Steward tried to no avail. By the time I took up the task my mother was weak and fragile and I didn't think she would be with us much longer. This was something she'd always felt was important to see finished. I spent hours, weeks, and months looking for the missing link that seemed to elude everyone in the family. I read book after book on the founding of towns and other books on first families in America. I read anything I could get my hands on that had to do with Early-American settlement. Eventually, after about four months, I found the missing link. Finally! I was gathering the proof and information to send off to the Mayflower Society of Descendants when something very surprising caught my eye. Every century someone in my family line would marry into my husband's family, all the way back to 1620. I hadn't taken my research much past the early 1600s, but from Keith and I all the way back to then, our families were connected. I also was able to connect his family coming over to America at the same time as mine. We shared the same grandfather 12 generations back.

When I told Keith about this and showed him what I had found in my research, he surprised me, saying, "I think you're right. I think we did meet in another life time. I think even in more than one lifetime."

I stood looking at Keith for a few moments after his comment, thinking back to how I said when we meant how I thought it wasn't the first time or spirits had been together. Then I thought there really might have been more truth in that statement then I thought at the time.

As I continued to compile my information and proof, I read anything and everything I could find on each of my direct ancestors back to 1620, learning about their voyage here and their lives through the generations and centuries here in America. As I read about some of them, I felt such a connection. It felt as if I knew them and was connected to them, as if I was reading a story about myself in another lifetime. Had my sixth sense become so in tune that I could even feel past lives with Keith? I had always seemed to have a strong awareness and sense of people and places and things that occurred to me and around me. This sensitivity was growing stronger as Keith and I grew closer. We seemed to be extensions of each other, always in tune to the other, sensing moods. Often we would both have the same thought, even when the topic was something unusual. We could be creating something in separate rooms, me expressing something on a canvas in one room, then walking into Keith's studio and find him sculpting the same thing in clay. At first it amazed us that we could be spontaneously creating the same ideas and thoughts in oil paints and clay without knowledge of the others idea or any thought of what they were trying to achieve. But as time went on, we grew accustomed to it. It was as natural as breathing to us.

Now that I was tied so closely to my family history, I often found myself wrapped up in the lives of my ancestor. I felt driven to find more about each and every generation. I started going through more old documents and pictures handed down through the family I came across in my closet. I had forgotten about the other box until I went looking for a throw cover on the top shelf of the closet. I would sit and read correspondence from one family member to another and feel as if I were with them, either reading or writing the correspondence I now held in my hands.

I felt so grateful to have found my soulmate and to have moved beyond the worries and doubts that most people face about marriage or their direction in life. To be as connected as we were, but still able to give each other space and independence without insecurities and fear, was a gift I tried to thoroughly appreciate. I passed people in the grocery store, wondering why some of them tried so hard to make eye contact with everyone that passes by them, are they still searching for their soulmate I asked myself. As if their spirit was still longing for the one true love. As if they were lost at sea, always searching for land. I have only to look into Keith's eyes to know that we have what some are still seeking. My soul and heart cry deep within for the lost souls still seeking to find their soulmates, hoping one day their souls will finally be filled and at peace.

I was deep in thought, reading correspondence from a great-great-great grandmother when the phone rang. The phone call was for Keith. A small town in Canada invited him to come and do a Bronze statue of the founder of their town. They wanted him to sculpt there so they could make sure every detail was done to their specifications. Keith told them he would be honored to go and create the sculpture, and they discussed the arrangements. After Keith got off the phone he shared the details and asked me to join him. I felt a real need to stay home and finish my genealogy research. I had a growing sense that my mother's time on earth is coming to an end and I wanted to finish the task before she passed.

Besides, I joke, "It's entirely too cold in Canada in the winter for me."

He laughed, "You're too thin-skinned."

Chapter Six

I spent the next week helping Keith gather the things he'd need for an indefinite stay. Creativity can't be put on a time limit; it would take as long as it needed to. The clients were to provide everything to create the sculpture, but he had a few special tools that he'd made that he knew he needed to take with him. After we got that taken care of, and the usual clothes and personal necessities packed, we spent the last few days just being together. We spent the time relaxing, making love, and a lot of time wandering the beach. We cherished the time we took together when we blocked out the rest of the world and focused on renewing the depth of our love. The day for his departure came quickly and I drove him to the airport. Early in our marriage we had promised each other that whenever we needed to be apart for work we would start the day talking to each other, even if we only had a few moments. We Skyped every morning and every evening before bed, allowing us to be face to face.

I spent the afternoon after he left reading correspondence, since the afternoon had brought in rain. I got so caught up in what I was reading that I lost track of time and it was late evening before I knew it. Hurriedly, I made a sandwich and showered, knowing Keith would be calling me soon. I had just picked up a book about my family when the phone rang. It was Keith, so I headed to my computer so we could see each other's faces. It was good to share our days and Keith told me about all the people he'd met.

I slept well in our bed even without Keith there. I could smell his scent all around me, as if that connected me to the rest of his being. It was not so for him. The next morning when we talked he told me as much.

"I miss you and our bed. I miss home," he said. "Would you send me something with your scent to help me sleep at night?" He rubbed his eyes.

"I can do that. Your scent in our bed helps me sleep, so I understand." I sipped the coffee I had made.

"Thanks. Tomorrow will be a long day of prepping everything before starting on the sculpture. I hate to cut talking with you short, but my driver will be here soon and I need to eat breakfast and meet more people before even going to the studio they have set up for me." He sounded tired and his hair was still wet from his shower.

"I understand. I appreciate even a few moments Skyping with you. I love you."

"I love you, too. Have a good day."

"You, too." I hung up the phone and took a bite of my croissant and then went onto the glassed in porch that overlooks the edge of the ocean.

I sat down and started reading about Richard and Elizabeth, one of the many great-grandparents Keith and I share. I suddenly started feeling the ocean pulling me to come out and get closer, to hear the waves crashing against its shore. I spent most of the day feeling as if something was drawing me out there. It was strange. I always loved living close to the shore, but never had I felt this sense of urgency to be right up on the ocean's edge. It felt terribly important. I gave in and spent the whole day at ocean's edge slowly making my way back to the house as early evening fell. I went in to warm by the fire and then take a hot shower. I had a quick dinner and some left over coffee as I wait for Keith to call.

I heard the Skype tones and rush to answer the call.

"Hi. How was your day?" I asked.

"Okay. The studio is nice, but it's not as comfortable as my own. It'll do for the project at hand. How was your day?" he asked. I could hear the tiredness in his voice, like it took much of his energy to get the words out.

"Well, it was strange. I felt this urgent call to the ocean's edge. I spent the day out there but nothing out of the ordinary happened."

"That's a bit disconcerting. Please, keep me informed if these unusual feelings, drawing you to the ocean's edge continue." Keith sounded tired and worn out even though he hadn't even begun the sculpting yet.

"I will. We should hang up so you can shower, eat and get to bed."

"You're probably right." He yawned. "I love you, Becca. Stay safe. I miss you so much already."

"I will. I miss you, too. I love you. Good night."

I liked it better when we expressed our love in person, but over the computer was no less heartfelt. Our ritual reminded me what a great life we have together and how connected we were. As the years passed, the connection deepened every year. I would sit and read by the fire until there is nothing more than warm embers in the fireplace and my eyes were heavy. I picked myself up from the chair and made my way to bed. I quickly fell to sleep, until morning woke me with the warm, welcomed light of the sun coming through the window pane.

I dressed and made my way to the kitchen where I made another pot of too much coffee. I forgot again that it was only me. This time I wrote myself a note for tomorrow. Keith called before I'd even finished my egg and toast breakfast. He wished me a good morning, and told me about his agenda for the day. I shared my plan to continue my research from the sun room, pushing through to get the proof I was looking for of our family connection to the *Mayflower*.

Yet, it wasn't long into the morning when I was again drawn to the ocean's edge. Staring out into the waves of an early November morning, I found a place to sit where I could watch the waves encroach on the shore as the tide rolled in. The winds picked up and grew stronger, taking over the sunny day. I slowly rose, bidding goodbye to the ocean and working my way home for the evening. I made plans to return again the next day, as if being beckoned to by an old friend far away.

Morning came early but I welcome it with excitement as I made my way to the ocean's edge once again. As the winter winds blew stronger and colder, and the waves rose higher. The draw to return became intensely stronger, even as I made my way there. I had a feeling as if I was waiting for someone to return to my side through the wind and waves from somewhere far away. Each day I spent on the shore seemed to end as fast as they came. Each evening I would sit by the fire, wondering where this strange calling came from. I was feeling that only continuing to walk the ocean's edge would bring me the answers I needed to find.

After another cold day of walking the shore, I fell asleep in front of the fire and morning found me in a hurry to dress and make my way to the ocean's edge yet again. I even opted out of breakfast to arrive earlier. I felt as if I might be missing whatever, or whoever, because of my timing. It was another day of wind and waves that grew stronger as the day progressed. Suddenly, I heard a voice from somewhere far away.

"Who are you? What do you want of me?" I called out into the wind and waves.

I wait, silently, for an answer. But, nothing came. The winds and the waves grew silent at the same time. The silence was deafening. I told myself to go home. It was probably nothing. It seemed silly to think I'd heard someone calling in the middle of the cold November winds. As I turned to walk away, I again thought I heard something and I stopped to listen. Again, I heard a voice calling out, a little louder now and as I stood, silent, I heard it over and over, growing stronger until I could make out what it was saying. It was a voice, but where could it be coming from? I turned to the ocean and could see the high tide rushing towards the shore as the wind grew stronger than ever before. Suddenly the voice was clear.

"Where is my love?"

I knew it couldn't be my husband; he had been out of town for weeks. I thought it must be someone further down the beach out of sight but whose voice carried with the wind. Again, I turned to leave when the voice called out again.

"My love, please don't leave! It is I. Oh, how I miss you, my love. How I long to be with you once again."

Suddenly, my perception shifts and I am in a scene from centuries past. I see a young couple standing on ocean's edge. Five young girls cling to their father as the women holds tight to his hand. It feels as though I am the one holding his hand and they are our children. I know that he is leaving and I see a tall ship with the words *Mayflower* on the side. This is not possible, I thought to myself. My many times great-grandparents, Richard and Elizabeth, had said goodbye to each other at ocean's edge the year he departed Plymouth, England for Plymouth, Massachusetts nearly four hundred years ago.

Richard squeezed Elizabeth's hand ever so tightly. "My love, time and tide and this lifetime and the ones to come will never keep our spirits away from each other long."

I could feel the love this couple had, so strong and deep. It was definitely the enduring soul deep love my mother had told me everyone could see shining out. I felt as though it was me saying goodbye to my soulmate, my heart and my spirit broke as he said goodbye. He tried to reassure her that they would be together again as soon as it was possible. I could feel her heart beating faster as their hand separated and he headed toward the tall ship. I could feel the tears run down her face as if they were running down mine. I tried to wipe them away from my face. I felt as if it were all happening to me, even as I knew that this exact scene had taken place between my grandparents many generations ago.

Richard boarded the tall ship. He stood at the deck railing, looking down upon his wife and daughters. He knew he would miss them and longed to be close to his wife, but he was steadfast in his belief that it was better to go first alone, Richard wanting to make sure this new world would realize his hopes for his family. That it would be safe, and that he could provide them a better life. Richard was sure they would be safe in England until that time came.

Elizabeth stood at the ocean's edge with their girls, waving to their father as the ship put out to sea. The daughters continued to wave until the ship was far from shore and could no longer see their father standing on the deck. Elizabeth fought back her tears of sorrow. It was the first time in their marriage they had been separated. Even before they married they had seen each other every day from the moment they met. As she stood watching her love sail away to the unknown new world, her thoughts went back to that day.

She and her sister had gone shopping on an early spring day and stopped to admire a dress hanging in Julia's Boutique. Richard and his friend, Robert were passing behind them. She turned to look at the tall young man at the same moment he noticed her. Their eyes met and time stood still for them. Neither one could look away, connected and staring. Elizabeth's sister called her name. Richard's friend called his. It was as if they were deaf. They watched in disbelief as light shined out from Richard and Elizabeth. They seemed entranced in silent conversation. Their companions just stood, watching, waiting, helpless to understand what was happening. After a few moments, Elizabeth's sister walked between them, breaking their eye contact. Questions about what had passed went unanswered.

Richard looked between his friend Robert and Elizabeth. "Good afternoon. My name is Richard. This is my friend, Robert. Would you ladies do us the honor of joining us for lunch?"

"We would love to, Richard," Elizabeth said before her sister, Mary had a chance to hesitate.

And that had been the beginning of their life together. Things moved quickly for the both of them. They never went a single day after meeting without spending time together. They were married soon after and before they knew it they had five beautiful little girls.

Elizabeth came back to the present thinking how quickly time had flown since that first meeting.

Her youngest daughter grabbed at her hand. They were still standing at the edge of the ocean but the ship had disappeared from site.

"Come on girls, it's time to go home." They quickly made their way to their carriage.

Richard's voyage was just beginning but his thoughts and concerns stayed with his wife and children. He wondered if he had made the right decision for himself, his family. He knew Elizabeth and the girls would be in safe and good hands staying with her father, but her father was old and wouldn't be on this earth many more years. He didn't want his wife and children to be alone in the world, having to fend for themselves. He wanted them to have the best of everything. That was why he was standing on the deck of *Mayflower*. It was a great opportunity to better their lives in a new world. He would be a merchant and build the first store in the new world. He knew there would be risks in taking on such an adventure, even in the best of circumstance, and these were far from the best. They were setting out late in the season, winter and harsh weather would soon be upon them. How would the ship hold up on such a voyage? Would they make it to land before the worst of the harsh winter winds? The questions and concerns were now flooding his mind with fears and regret. *How could I leave my Elizabeth?* It had seemed like a much more inviting opportunity when he was standing on the shore. There was no turning back now, he would have to make the best of the voyage and what lay ahead. There was no point in letting his thoughts and fears get the best of him.

I must keep my mind busy and my body active.

He quickly found a place below deck to store his things and to make a bed for himself. He had many books with him. He sat down on the palette bed he had made and started reading. Once he felt settled again he got up and joined a group of the other passengers making plans for landing, determining how they would structure their new settlement. Richard put himself forward to be friendly and was quickly accepted into their group. Every day the men would sit and talk of the new lives ahead of them and what was expected of each and every one. They all agreed that they had to stay united in their quest in order to make it work. Day after day they met, shoring up their plans.

The long voyage was starting to get the best of many. Some were growing weak and sick. The weather was not in their favor. Fewer men gathered at the table every day. Those who weren't sick provided care for those who were. By the time they reached shore, some were laying below deck, too weak to even come up to see their new land. Worse, they had not landed at their intended destination but were much further north. They agreed that day to write their Compact. Most of the passengers signed it. Richard and others agreed they needed to go ashore and find out what lay ahead of them, so the strongest amongst them went and scouted out the land. The ground was frozen beneath their feet as they walked. The winds of winter were strong upon them. Richard soon let his thoughts wander back to his wife and children. His confidence was shaken by the barren landscape. This destination no longer seemed like the right path for his family's journey through life. How could he ever bring them to this vast, cold wilderness? Would he ever see them again? The ocean and time that parted them seemed insurmountable for a moment, before he rallied himself. Whatever it took, he would do. He was going to make, not just a life, but a better life, here, for his children and his Elizabeth. There was no other choice.

The scouting party had been out most of the day and planned on another trip to land tomorrow. The sunlight was fading quickly as they made their way back to the ship to report what they had found. They would be returning to land again the next day to choose a spot to build on. It was the dead of winter and many were sick and dying. The number of men who were still strong amongst them dwindled each day. Those who were not ill lacked strength from poor nutrition, but they kept forging ahead, more determined than ever to make it work. Richard saw not only men ill and dying, but also women and children. He was glad he had chosen not to bring his Elizabeth with him even though he missed her presence fiercely.

It will be better when they have something to come to besides frozen ground and dwindling supplies. I could never recover if I lost Elizabeth or my girls to sickness and death. As long as I have breath in my body, I will make this work.

He had been overwhelmed, watching three men take a whole day to dig a shallow grave to lay women and children. Richard decided it was time, not for thought, but for action. He and the men with enough strength still in their bodies decided that the next day they would start building. The plan was to build a meeting house first. Each day they worked long and hard and before long they could see their meeting house taking shape. By now the harsh winter had turned to early spring. Only about half of the people who had made the journey survived the winter. Everyone who made it was determined they would succeed and thrive in their new home. The *Mayflower* had stayed close to shore all winter, but now was making ready to return to England. No one went back, all but the sailors stayed in the new world, their new home.

Richard sent a letter back for Elizabeth. He knew she would have worried all winter and would be waiting for word from him. He sat down alone with pen in hand and started to write.

My love, my Elizabeth, how I miss you and long to have you by my side again.

But the time is not yet arrived to have you come to me. It was a long, hard, cold winter. I am doing well and the winter winds have finally subsided. The winds bring a gentle breeze from the south now. I work from the time I rise until I return to my bed late in the night. We have built a meeting house and the first house for a family. It will be another year before we can even begin on the house that will one day be our home. It was agreed we would build first according to need. Those with wives and children already here will get the first houses built. I could not argue the decision and I know you would not in your care for our own

children. The time will come and we will have a

house for our family. But until that time, my love, it

is better you wait in England. Food has been

scarce, but with spring upon us there is hope of

planting a garden for all to share. I will send word

with every ship that comes to let you know how I am

and the progress I have made toward building us a

home.

I hope this letter finds you and the children

well. Give them all hugs from me and tell them all I

love and miss them. My Elizabeth, how I miss you

and wish you were by my side. I miss your touch,

your lips, and your loving arms. I miss everything

about you my love. I find you amongst my dreams

more often than not. I always wake feeling

comforted by your visit. You look into my eyes and

*see deep within my soul, as though you come to
bring me strength. It heartens me to feel you with
me, my sweet Elizabeth. The day will come though,
that we will be together again. I, like you, wish it
could be sooner than later, but it must be like this a
while longer my love.*

*I wait to hear back from you and to know
how well you and the children have fared since I
have been away. Send letters with any ship heading
this way, my love, for I hunger for any word from
you. There is a man by the name of William
Bradford here that keeps a journal and he writes in
it every day. I don't know if he writes of me much,
or at all. I think he writes mostly of the people he
traveled here with and their daily lives and
struggles. He is a nice enough man and has been a
great help with making sure everyone contributes to*

the common good. One day I will introduce you to

him. I will not say that building this new life is easy.

It has not been and will stay so for quite some time.

But I have high hopes for this new world and the

life we will have together here one day. Don't give

up hope. Have courage and strength for the

children and for me, my love.

All my heart and soul,

Richard

It was many months after he wrote that

Elizabeth finally received Richard's letter. Every

time Elizabeth heard of a ship heading into port she

was there, hoping that Richard had changed his

mind and was coming back to her, or that there

would finally be word from him, calling to her to

come to him. She could not help but worry that he

might not have survived the trip. She had heard nothing in eight long months. Deep within Elizabeth's soul she believed she would know if he were gone forever. Finally, that one ship came. She asked her father to watch after the children while she went to see if there was any word of Richard. She hoped with everything within her that he would be on the ship. But, he wasn't. The captain handed her a letter and also personally reassured her he was well. Elizabeth thanked the captain, and with letter in hand she made her way to a bench. She wanted a few minutes undisturbed to read and savor his every word. She wanted to pretend he was by her side and they were alone in a private moment. She opened the letter and held it in her hands for several moments, as if it was his hand she was holding, before she even read one word.

It was almost regretful that she slowly unfolded the letter and started to read, clinging to each word like someone holding onto the last breath in their body before death takes them away. She sat and read the letter over and over. She cried. She had been strong the whole time he had been gone. The sudden release of finally having word softened her and left her weak with longing to have him by her side. For so many years he had been her strength and her comfort. She pictured in her mind the harsh winter they endured and how many lives had been lost. It could have easily been Richard who died. She quickly discarded the thought so it would not consume her and leave her too emotional when she returned to face her children. She clung to the good news in the letter, and to the dreams Richard still held. She thought of his dreams for this new world.

She could hear his hopes of building their life as a family there.

She slowly got up and made her way home. She told the children their father missed them and sent his love and hugs. She then sat to write a letter back to him to send on the next ship heading to the new colony. She wrote to Richard of her love for him and stories about how the girls were doing and that everything at home was fine. She kept her letter cheerful and her news positive. Knowing her sorrow at being apart from him would only make his task harder and tear at his heart.

She took her letter down to the port and gave it to the port master, asking that he give it to the captain of the first ship heading to New

Plymouth. She told him her husband had gone eight months ago.

Returning home, she sat alone for the longest time. She reflected on their lives together and how happy they had always been. She reminded herself that he had never let her down and always did everything he said he would, both for her and for their family. Elizabeth had always believed in him before, and today would not be the day she gave up. She would stay positive and hope as he did. She also prayed that they would soon be together rather than later. She longed for the day he sent for her. Richard took this chance to start a fresh in the new world in hopes of being the merchant everyone went to for their goods. Richard and his brother, Benjamin and his cousin, William had already worked out all the details for the business before Richard set sail. Benjamin and William would handle everything on their end an England and Richard would handle everything in New Plymouth.

Elizabeth got up and busied herself from that day forward. She would visit Richard in her dreams every night, but during the day she refused to let herself get lost in thought and worry. It wouldn't do any of them any good. It was a difficult resolution to keep. It was over a year before she heard from Richard again.

My love, how I miss your touch, your smile, your beautiful green eyes. I miss the way you speak my name. I miss everything about you my dearest. I am getting ever closer to the day when it will be right for you and the children to join me in

Plymouth, New England. It is the thought of you
and the children that drove me to push forward as
quickly as possible to make a home and life for you.
I take long walks down to the ocean's edge in the
evening after a long day's work. I stand there and
reach out for you, hoping the wind and waves will
carry my love back to you. I hope you can hear my
voice, carried by the wind. My next letter will
instruct you to join me.

From that day forward Elizabeth went each
evening to the ocean's edge to call back to her love.
She thought, if I only stand quiet, then I will hear
his calls to me. She found the daily practice to be a
huge comfort. She felt as if every night drew them a
little closer, even though the depth and length of the
ocean kept them from each other's side.

It was another year and a half more before she heard back from Richard. She had continued her practice of meeting every ship that made port in hope of his return, or a letter. Finally, the day came. When she made her way down to the port there was a letter from her Richard. She was so filled with excitement she could hardly contained herself.

My love, how I miss and long for you. The day has come for you to ready yourself and the girls and come to me. I cannot wait to hold you in my arms again and kiss your sweet lips. Hurry my love. Come with the next ship.

She couldn't believe what she was reading! Finally, he was telling her to come to him. She went to the bench where she had sat before and read it over and over again.

"The day has arrived! I will be with my Richard again," she said to the ocean.

She got up and ran home as fast as she could make her way. She told the girls of the news from their father and sent them to begin preparations. Then she went back down to the port and got the information on the next ship leaving for New Plymouth. It would only be three weeks. She booked passage for them all. She didn't want to wait. It could fill up. She didn't want to chance having to wait for another ship before she and her five girls could make the journey together. The children were excited to see their father again. They had missed him for so long. They had all grown a great deal and couldn't wait to share their many stories with him. The two oldest were becoming young ladies, but acted like small children at the thought of seeing their father. They couldn't wait to hear of his adventures in building a new life for them all.

The day finally came. They boarded *Ann* that would take Elizabeth to her husband's waiting arms. The trip would be long, but unlike Richard's voyage, the weather was in their favor. She and the children would step off the ship with a place to go to, unlike Richard and the rest who had struggled to even make it through the first winter. How long she had waited for this day to come, to sail off the shores of England and join her Richard. She gave little thought to the many things she would be leaving behind. Only her father and brother mattered to her. Everything else she would leave behind seemed so unimportant compared to rejoining Richard. As they left port and sailed away,

Elizabeth breathed a sigh of relief. She knew Richard would be standing at the ocean's edge, waiting for her and the children to join him. She hoped the journey would be smooth and swift.

She knew the voyage wouldn't be easy. The boat was full with people wanting to start a new life in New Plymouth. Some days went by quickly, while others seemed to drag. Long rainy days were the worst, with everyone packed into the hold. Still, Elizabeth managed to make the best of it, reading to her children and brushing their hair for them. Weeks went by and finally they were getting close to their destination. Everyone on board was ready for the voyage to end.

Elizabeth felt that no one was more excited than she, not even her children. She had missed

Richard so much and for so long. Her spirit seemed different, weaker, without him by her side. The special connection they had renewed itself when they gazed into each other's eyes, and filled her being with pure love and joy. How she missed that special bond, looking into his eyes and feeling his arms gently wrap around, drawing her closer until their bodies connected to each other like their souls. She had not dared to think of those moments while they had been separated so far apart from each other. She didn't want her thoughts of those moments to consume her without the real possibility of having him come to her. But with land in sight, she knew he would be waiting to take her in his arms and look into her eyes, connecting deep down into her soul and filling her with his love. Before she could give another thought to how much longer it would be, they approached the shore. The crew lowered small boats to take people to the shore. She hurriedly got the girls together. She wanted them to be on the first boat. Others were quickly getting in line behind her and the girls. She stood firm in place with the girls, showing she was steadfast in her decision to be on the first boat. No one questioned her. Finally, the captain gave orders to the crew to start loading the boats. They filled quickly.

Elizabeth fussed with her hair and straightened her dress. Then she fussed over the girls, making sure they too would look their best. The boat crossed the distance, heading toward a cluster of people waiting at the shoreline. Everyone had turned out to greet the family and friends they had left behind. Elizabeth scanned the shore, looking for a glimpse of Richard. When she finally

found him, he had already located her among the
passengers on that small boat. At that moment their
eyes connected. Richard hurried to the boat as they
made shore. He came straight to her and the girls to
help them out. Then, with Elizabeth and his girls on
shore, he took Elizabeth into his arms in the way
they had both craved. He hugged her so tight he
thought he might crush her as he kissed her soft
cheek. Then he pulled himself back and looked
deeply into her eyes so they could replenish their
souls, connecting once again to his darling
Elizabeth. He then had a hug for each of his girls as
he told each one how he had missed them and
admired how each had grown over their years apart.

Greetings complete for the moment, he took
Elizabeth by the hand and led them to their new
home. He promised to return to shore to collect their

belonging after all the passengers had debarked. The boats would be busy for a while just ferrying people.

Richard was glad the weather was warmer than at his landing. It let Elizabeth and the girls take time to stretch their legs and get steadiness of solid land under their feet again as they slowly walked to their new home. It was a beautiful day. The weather was warm, but not too warm. There was a gentle breeze, just enough to be glad to have it come across your face. As they walked along, all the girls were trying to talk to their papa at once, they had missed him so. Elizabeth remained quiet, letting the girls have their time with him. They asked millions of questions as they walked and Richard tried to answer as fast as he could. He was beaming with pure love and joy to have Elizabeth by his side again and he held her hand in his as they walked.

She too was beaming, her soul at peace again with Richard by her side. His voice had always resonated deep within her soul, calming and comforting her.

Before long, he was pointing at the small village and saying, "That one right there is our house."

Elizabeth squeezed his hand at *our house*. How she had longed to have a home again with him. Their place in England had seemed to be a shell when Richard was gone. Nothing would be a home to her without Richard.

As they made their way to the door, Richard said, "Girls, your mother gets to go in first. I want her to be the first to see what I have built for our family." He let go of Elizabeth's hand to open the door for her, his face beamed brighter than before as they walked into their home. She looked around, trying to take in everything around her.

"I love it, Richard. I couldn't have dreamt of anything nicer."

The girls made their way in behind them. They were just as pleased as their mother. Truly, Elizabeth was happy just to be with Richard again, no matter where or how they lived as long as it was together. The girls and Elizabeth were tired from the long voyage but, still giddy with the excitement of arrival. They were eager to wash and put on fresh clothes. Elizabeth brought a small satchel with a change of clothes for each off the boat with them.

They knew it would not be until tomorrow before the rest of their things would come off the ship. Richard gave them a bar of lye soap and brought up buckets of water for them all. He then went outside so Elizabeth and the girls could wash. When they were freshly bathed and clothed, Richard emptied the large basin of water.

Then the proud husband and father took Elizabeth and the girls around to some of their new neighbor's houses to be introduced. How he longed for this day to come. Richard and Elizabeth never missed a beat, expressing deep from within their souls that their love for each other was just as strong as ever. Now, back together again, it was as if they hadn't been apart at all. They were able to find a routine that suited all of them quickly. If there was anything different, it was that everything seemed to come easier for them. Things they might have found difficult before were somehow lessened by having the other one close.

Elizabeth and Richard later had two more children together, two boys. Everything was going much better in both of their lives now that they were back together and raising their children. The business Richard was building was starting to take root and cargo for the general store they built was coming in on a regular basis now with more and more ships that seemed to be coming to the shores of Plymouth now. Richard knew now was the time to start bringing Elizabeth to the meetings the town's men had once a week to conduct business. Even though at first the men in the meetings objected strongly, Richard would not give in and send Elizabeth home. He told everyone Elizabeth was his partner not just in marriage but in his business, also. Over the next months and years not only did they get used to her in the meeting they grew to like her attending. She could tell some we're still a little taken back, but only a few.

Five years had now come and gone when Richard fell ill. His faith was sealed. Richard was dying. He knew it and so did Elizabeth. She sat by his side, tending to his every need. Both of their souls knew that they were about to part from each other. Richard couldn't stand the thought of leaving his Elizabeth alone in life to finish raising their children, in a new world to make it on her own. He knew Elizabeth would never remarry. He knew that she knew he was dying and not long in this world. Richard always looked many steps ahead in life. That was why he had Elizabeth at every meeting; he wanted the men to be comfortable around her and to grow used to her being there. He knew if something happened to him, he wanted her to be already accepted by the men, that they knew she had a business sense about her as much as any of them. He didn't want to think of her alone with their children, trying to fend for their selves or being a burden in this new world. He wanted her to be an asset that the people would go to get their supplies from in the new world, instead of seeking someone else out for the job.

Richard and his younger brother we're close and he knew his brother, Benjamin wouldn't let him down either. He and Richard were in business together along with his cousin, William. His brother and William were still in England and took care of the supply chain there. Richard would write and let his brother know the supplies they needed and they would send them. His brother and cousin never had let him down and he knew they wouldn't let Elizabeth down either. Richard had made sure Elizabeth knew everything he knew from the moment she stepped off the *Ann*. He left nothing out and showed her exactly how to manage every part of the trade until it became second nature to her. He had managed to accumulate ten more acres of land and even some cows and chickens over the years. So even though he never wanted to leave Elizabeth, he knew he didn't have much time left. He told her how much he loved her and the children. Mary, the oldest had already married so had Ann and Sarah, but all lived close enough to be there in a few minutes. He knew she and the children would be fine. He told her that his life on earth was ending and if there was any chance they could meet in another lifetime he would find her somehow.

Then, Richard took a one last deep breath. Elizabeth laid her head upon his chest and sobbed over the loss of her Richard. Then, she got up and had Joseph, their youngest son go get a few of Richard's friends to come get his body and bury him. Nathaniel, their oldest son went and got his sisters. Before Joseph returned with some of Richard friends, Timothy, Michael, and Daniel she called all her children into the room to say goodbye to their father. Now with Richard gone she knew she could never show weakness again. She would have to stand strong and forge forward in life alone. She knew what Richard wanted her to do and she was going to do exactly that. As more and more people and ships came into the new world she was ready to be the one everyone came to for all their merchandising needs and she did just that. Elizabeth finished raising their children on her own except for the help of the older girls. She was starting to teach her children the trade just as Richard had her. Richard's brother and cousin were also teaching their children their part of trade so that the next generation would be equipped to takeover and handle the business smoothly without anyone from the outside realizing they had transitioned from one generation to the next, until it had long since been done.

Elizabeth grew the business into what she knew Richard wanted without bending or caving to anyone. She was a force to be reckoned with. Now her and Richard's children we're doing the same. A few people tried soon after Richard's death to take over and run her out, but to no avail. Now, nobody even attempted that, not even with their children running the business. Elizabeth watched as her and Richards's children all grew into adulthood, having their own children. Elizabeth felt fortunate that all their children had lived into adulthood since many of her friends had lost children throughout the years. Then Elizabeth paused to realize she had grown old, very old. She thought at first she wouldn't make it through the first days, then weeks, months, and the first year when Richard died. She thought, were did all the time go? She was so old and gray and worn out. She no longer worked with the business. The children had completely taken over and every one of their children we're doing great. Her grandchildren were now being taught the family business by her children. Elizabeth felt weak and tired, but decided to take a walk to the ocean's edge.

As she walked to the ocean, she thought about how time and life had passed since they were reunited on the beach, and how happy and excited she was to finally get to be with her Richard again. She thought how she was once again missing Richard more than ever. She missed his arms around her, the love they showed even without speaking. Just to have him in the same room with her made everything within her being feeling complete and whole. It had been many years since she had that feeling within her. The closer she got to the shore the more she thought of Richard. She reached the shore and it was as if he was there with her again.

She was tired from the walk and found a large rock to sit on as she gazed out at the ocean. The waves were gentle and slowly coming ashore. She thought she could hear Richard once again, calling her in the wind and waves as they did when they were separated by the ocean. *I'm sure I can hear him talking, calling me to come to him, to be with him again.* He missed her and wanted to be with her again. As she sat upon the rock, listening to him calling her as the waves met the shore, she felt strange. She felt as if her soul was leaving her body to reunite with her Richard. The next morning a fishermen found Elizabeth's body upon the rock. She had left her old worn out body upon the rock.

Chapter Seven

Suddenly, I feel the waves cover my feet and I'm shivering as I stand at ocean edge with the sun fading fast. I head toward home to warm myself by the fire. I sat and thought about the day and how it made me feel. It was as if I had been taken back to another time and place somehow. My first thought was that I had fallen asleep, but I remembered I had been standing when it had all taken place. *What happened? Could I somehow be in two places at once, or was I just daydreaming?* I decided I must have been daydreaming. As I got up from the fireplace hearth and busied myself with dinner, warm bath, and bed. I fell asleep as soon as I laid my head on the pillow.

The morning sun woke me and I crawled out of bed, but as soon as my feet hit the floor I was ready to start my day at the ocean's edge. But with Keith gone and my heart, soul and body missing him, craving his voice, his touch, and smile. I decided to call him this morning just to let him know how much I am missing him before he called me. Then I would be off to the beach, I had to figure out if the day before had been a daydream, or if something else had happened. Rushing out, I found a place to sit, and thought about my husband's soon return from his business trip.

Again, I heard the voice calling, "My love, I am here! I miss you and love you. Come to me."

Again, I could see a woman, her heart beating faster with excitement as she looked over the bow of a boat. She was waiting her turn to come to shore. As their eyes met, I could feel their souls fill up and their troubled spirits quiet as their eyes stayed fixed upon each other. Even on this bright sunny day, the light coming from within them shone brighter. If a total eclipse of the sun had darkened the sky, and the only light on earth would come from their two souls joining together; it would still be as bright as day. Neither could see anything but the other for a moment in time as their souls found each other.

I felt as if I were that woman from centuries past. That I was not dreaming, but remembering a past life I lived long ago, brought back by the winds and the tides. Although this was a different memory than before, my spirit knew this life. It was now clear that this wasn't a dream, but a recalling of memories. I wonder, why now? What is causing this window into my spirit's former lives, where I am taken to another century? Again, I am at the ocean's edge, standing on the shore just having disembarked from a ship. A man reached out to help me get my footing as I stepped onto the shore. Our eyes met and our spirits connected, as though they had been together many lifetimes. I knew in that moment I had met the man I would spend the rest of my life with. I knew the bonds of time had connected us long before the moment when I stood waiting for my luggage to be transferred to shore.

The man I was drawn to starts talking to my brother, who I had come to see. They already knew each other. My brother introduced us as our eyes met once again.

He reached out to take my hand into his and said, "How was your voyage?"

Before I could answer, he invited my brother and me to dine with him that evening. My brother took one look at us, his friend still holding my hand, and explained that after my long voyage it would be better if he joined us for dinner the next day instead. With another look at our joined hands, his brother Stephen urged his friend, Nathaniel, to come help him with my baggage, requiring him to relinquish my hand. We parted reluctantly, looking forward to the next day.

Nathaniel arrived the next morning before we had sat for breakfast. From my room, I could hear Nathaniel and my brother discussing me. My brother made his way to the door of my bedroom and knocked.

"Cecelia, you have company."

I could tell by his voice he was uncomfortable, and I knew that Nathaniel would be there when I opened the door. My eyes meet his as he stood in the hallway beside my brother.

"Nathaniel has something to ask you," my brother said.

"Cecelia, I laid awake all night waiting for daylight to come so I could ask you to be my bride, my wife. As long as I have breath in this body I will love you, and in every life after this one, until the end of time. My spirit leapt as our eyes first met and the moment I took your hand in mine, I knew it was meant to be in no other. I felt our spirits connect that very moment—"

"Yes!" I interrupted, before he could say another word. "When will we be married?"

"Today, if you would like."

"Yes," I said, as my brother stood by my side. I thought he would be shocked or angry, but instead he acted as though he expected it. "Brother, does this not surprise you?"

"No, I could see yesterday that you to we're meant for each other. There was no hiding the love you two had from the moment you met. The light that shines from both of you is incredibly bright. I knew Nathaniel would ask you, and you would say yes. I have to confess. I expected him to show up in the middle of the night with a preacher in tow," he chuckled.

"The preacher is outside," Nathaniel said. "I was waiting for Cecelia's answer before I called him into your house."

Nathaniel and I married right then and my brother helped Nathaniel load my luggage onto his buggy. As we travelled the road to our home as husband and wife, I felt as if my spirit had been calling me to Nathaniel, calling me from the other side of the ocean through the wind and the waves. The moment I saw my beloved Nathaniel, I knew he was the longing and calling I was hearing from my home on the other side of the ocean. Certain I would forever be his wife. Time and tide and wind and waves have brought our two spirits together.

I saw a house in the distance before Nathaniel could say, "My love, there is our home ahead of us, where we will raise our children together and grow old by each other's side."

"Nathaniel, I feel as though I have already known you a lifetime. How wonderful life is that we have found each other early in our lives. We will have many babies together." We embraced each other, drawing closer as we drew near our home.

As we reached the house, Nathaniel got out of the buggy and gently reached for my hand, then caught my sides as he swung me down. Before I knew it, I was cradled in his arms as he carried me into the house. Crossing the threshold, he kept me in his arms and kissed me ever so passionately as he took me to the bedroom and laid me upon the bed.

He slowly climbed on top of me, undressing me even as he kept kissing me upon my lips and face, down my neck. I was in a haze of sensation and hardly realized he had my dress unbuttoned down to my waist. Now he was kissing my breasts and tenderly caressing them. I was completely overcome with the feelings of passion we felt for each other. Caressing, he lifted my skirt and slowly and gently entered inside my body. I got lost in the passion. In the moment when we both exploded with our love for each other, he fell into my arms. He rolled us to our sides to hold each other, arms entwined, and looked into each other's eyes with more unity than I thought two people could have for one another. I knew that our life together had truly begun. We would forever be connected, not only one in spirit but body. I knew we would have a great life together.

The days and years flew by. We had six children in six years and we loved them. We looked forward to having many more as we walked down life's path together as one.

Rumors of war started coming frequently. They were calling it a revolution to separate from the King and England. My brother brought more news every day of what was going on in town and what plans were being made. Soon Nathaniel started going to the meetings to be a part of the great revolution that was about to take place. Nathaniel and my brother were friends with George Washington. Nathaniel was also one of the best riders to ever mount a horse, and everyone knew this to be true.

Rumors of war turned to actuality. Nathaniel left us to go to Bunker Hill to fight. When next I heard from him, he had been made Major by General George Washington. After a long fought war with many lives and years gone by, Nathaniel returned home to me. Our hearts had not missed one beat away from each other. Our souls were again one. As he had done that first day of our lives together, Nathaniel carried me to our bedroom and made love to me, allowing us to once again be one in body as our souls always were.

We were still as much in love as the day we had met; when our eyes met for the first time and our souls connected at the ocean's edge. Our

Children Cornelia, Christopher, Johnathan had grown in what seemed an instant to Nathaniel.

"I can't believe they have gotten so big while I have been gone. It seems as if it were only yesterday that we were welcoming them into this world and teaching them to walk and talk," he said to Cecilia. "Now they have hopes and dreams of their own to follow. They are growing into fine people. I'm just thankful I'm home in time to see the younger ones finish growing. I didn't plan to be gone so long, my Cecelia. I missed you every day and longed to be with you. My thought was that freedom would come quickly and we would all be home in only a few months. I certainly didn't think it would be years. I will not leave you again for anything. My soul could not bear the loneliness of an absence from you again. With each passing day I was losing the strength to carry on without you. My soul is always hungry for you."

Cecelia knew just how he felt. She had longed for him as much. She had dreamt of the day he would come home to stay and not leave her again. Now, with the new found freedom of their country and its independence from England, she had peace from deep within her soul. Nathaniel was home to stay. They were filled with peace and happiness, knowing somehow that they would not have to endure another separation.

As their lives settled back into a comfortable routine, they watched their remaining children grow. Years went by and they watched as the children left, one by one, to make their own way in life, but none went too far. As their children started to have children, they were there to watch them grow and to enjoy their grandchildren as they had enjoyed their own young children.

But, peace turned to tragedy as Ely their youngest grandchild only of few months old died of pneumonia. Their daughter Cornelia was devastated by the loss of Ely. No comfort was found for their daughter, Cornelia, from her husband, Luke, or her other children Isaac and Althea. Her arms ached to hold her son, Ely. Nothing could satisfy her arms. Her other children would climb onto her lap and she would pray that they would satisfy her, but as she hugged them the pain stayed. She physical hurt from the pain. She felt as if part of her soul had left her; she knew she would never be whole again.

Cecelia wanted nothing more than to take the hurt and pain from her daughter and bare it for her. But she was helpless knowing as much as she wanted to be able to do this for her daughter, she couldn't. All she could do was pray for the day God would ease the pain deep within her daughter's soul. Days, months and years went by before Cecelia saw a healing going on in her daughter. Cecelia rejoiced silently not wanting to bring back any memory that might bring back the hurt and pain her daughter had endured for so long.

Cecelia knew time would help Cornelia move on, but that Cornelia would never forget and live the rest of her life with a peace of her heart and soul gone for the rest of her days on earth. Cecelia and Nathanial often found themselves sitting on the porch now more than not, reflecting on the hurt and the pain their Cornelia had suffered and endured. Grateful that they had not had to endure the same pain first hand themselves. Even though they felt they would have suffered it and carried the burned themselves than to have watched their daughter go through such undescribed pain within her soul. Cecelia, even though she was Ely's grandmother and Cornelia mother, and felt pain and heartache for Cornelia, she knew that it didn't come close to what her daughter was going through. Cecelia thought, you hear, see, and want to understand the pain a mother feels at the loss of their child so you can comfort them. But the pain is so great that they alone feel it.

Comfort seems to never come, only time seems to lessen the pain, but it's burned into them forever more. The birthdays never celebrated. The smiles never seen. The hugs never gotten. The word mommy never heard. The question who would he look like? What color eyes and hair would he have? How tall would he have been? What and who would he have become? The horrible day that he died that came once a year to awaken the pain felt the moment he died.

Cecelia stop herself from thinking anymore about it at that moment. She fell to her knees and pray out loud, "My Lord, heal my daughter. Take away her heartache. I want to see her happier, smiling more, and hope in my lifetime to hear her laugh again. I love the laugh you gave her, Lord." Cecelia thought, I almost feel her pain and I turned away from it and fell to my knees in prayer to you my Lord.

Then Cecelia got up off her knees and went to visit her daughter. The first thing she did was tell Cornelia she loved her and gave her a mother's warm, gentle hug, and then as they separated, she said, "Let's go outside and watch Isaac and Althea play."

They sat on the porch, neither talking, just watching the children be children. When Isaac fell and came crying with a hurt knee to his mama. Something about that cry of help stirred something in Cornelia. She ran to Isaac as he was running to her. She picked him up into her arms and wiped away his tears and told him he would be okay now. She sat down on the porch, holding Isaac close and started to make funny faces at him until he laughed and, she laughed.

In that moment, she realized she had two beautiful children that loved and needed their mama and she would have to return to life and the living and be the best she could be for her Isaac and Althea. Cecelia smiled as she watched her daughter return. She knew then Cornelia would be okay. Over the years, Isaac and Althea would bring much joy to Cornelia. But on Ely's birthday and the anniversary of his death, Cornelia would always announce she was taking a walk and would disappear into the woods for a couple of hours and return tired and wore out. Nobody ever questioned or ask to go with her. She wanted and needed that time to herself to reflect back on her Ely. She felt she needed to allow herself that time because he was special. He was her son. He meant something to her. He might have only lived a few months but every day of those months meant something to her. His life mattered and was important, only short. She thought of Ely every day but only in passing. She didn't want to dwell and cause herself pain. She reserved a few hours on two days of the year for him and him alone. Cecelia felt the Lord had answered her prayers that day.

The last I saw of Nathaniel and Cecelia, they are sitting on their front porch. Many years had passed. They had grown old together, and still they felt as if they were one in thought, mind, and body.

Now the waves of the ocean brushed the shore and brought me back to the present. I still don't know the reason I am having these glimpses back in time to other lives. I feel I have lived through each of the centuries myself. I thought that perhaps it must be from all the reading about the past lives of my ancestor. It would make sense. I had been through so much history and correspondence between family members. Holding the documents that they held in their hands and had taken pen to, it must have stirred old memories deep in my soul. Despite my early start, the day was ending as I came back to myself. I headed toward the house as I said goodbye to the day. As I made it to the door, I heard my computer; Keith was calling. I hurried into the house to answer and hear the sweet love of my life.

"Hello," he said. "I thought I'd call you earlier tonight. I was missing you something terrible. You have been strong on my mind all day as I worked. I felt like you were calling out to me. I just had to call and talk to you, my love, and tell how much I miss you and long to be with you. How are you? How has your day been?"

"Keith, I have been having the strangest thing going on since you've been gone," I said.

"Tell me, what is going on?"

"Every day I've felt a strong call out to the ocean's edge. It's some voice from the past, and then I find myself seeing a past life we have lived together. It has been amazing to glimpse into the lives we lived together, generations, and centuries past."

"I can't wait 'til I am home again and we're in each other's arms and you can tell me all about the past lives we've lived. Were we as happy in the past as we are now?"

"We're as amazingly happy as we are now, but I think we seem more complete in our life now than in the past. It's like, with each life we've reached another level of oneness. We get closer with each century than the one before."

"I guess that is why you have weighed so heavy on my mind today, my love. It's our souls connecting in the past while we're here in the present moment. Did I tell you today how much I love you?"

"Yes. This morning, and I feel it even with you so far away," I said, as I finished up my bite of food and putting the dishes in the sink.

"About that, I wish I had thought this out a little more before I said, yes. I don't like being away from you for even one night, let alone who knows how many."

"I know. Me either, babe. I guess I have the advantage of at least being back in our home with the scent of you all around me. That reminds me, did you get the scarf I wear yet?

"I did, thank you. I laid it on the pillow next to the one I use. I can't say it helps a lot, but it does help some. I smell it every night before closing my eyes and in the morning when I awake. I'm putting everything I have into this statue but I needed to talk with you. Nothing seems to inspire my creative side more than being close to you," Keith said.

"I understand, babe. Take pictures of what you have done so far and maybe the thought of showing me will help inspire you."

"I'll try that. It might help some," he said. "I know I finished a little earlier today and I should've worked longer. It would've gotten me home to you a couple hours sooner. But I did work hard and I just had to see your face and tell you how my whole being misses you, heart, body, and soul."

"I miss you, too. I think missing you so much has triggered my visits back into the past."

"I feel so much better after seeing and talking to you. I think I'll have an early dinner, hot shower, and make my way to bed to try and get a long, full-night's sleep. I really haven't been getting that without you by my side. I wake up and feel for you every night, and I wake up when my arm hits an empty spot where you should be beside me."

"I hope you are able to get your creative thoughts flowing more freely and that the skill of your hands will fall into the clay with direction my sweet, gentle love. I will get off here so you can get that early dinner and shower and get to bed."

"Goodnight, my love. Sweet dreams. I will talk to you in the morning."

"Goodnight babe, I love you with every ounce of my being."

I tossed a log on the fire and went to take a shower. I came back through the living room in my comfy sleepwear, heading to the kitchen for something easy. Grilled ham and cheese and a cup of hot soup was sounding good for a quick supper. I sat in the kitchen at the counter to eat, and then cleaned up the kitchen and made my way back into the living room. I picked up one of the many old documents littering the room and I looked up at the painting I had done, 17 years ago now, of the old man of the sea. It seemed like a life time ago and yet, just yesterday that we hung it there.

Keith and I enjoy the life we made together. As in everyone's life there have been struggles to overcome. Like when Sean had been out riding his motorcycle and blue skies suddenly turned to clouds and rain. Sean hit a slick spot of oil on the road and the bike slipped out from under him and he hit his head on the road so hard it broke his neck and killed him.

It was hard for me to get passed Sean's death. Sean had called that morning wanting Keith to go riding with him. But Keith was busy finishing a Sculpture for a client. I talked to Sean for a few minutes and hoped he would find someone to go with him. Sean and I were close friends before I met Keith, but after meeting Keith, Sean grew even closer in heart. For I believe that Sean played a big role in me finding Keith. I will always have a special place in my heart reserved for memories of Sean. Keith and I grew stronger and closer through struggles. They made us realize how short life really is and to hold close those that are near and dear to us.

After reflecting over the past as I was looking at the painting hanging on the wall, I turned my attention to the document in my hand and thought it may have been partly the scent that lingered in the paper that brought back these memories of past lives. Keith and I felt comforted by the scent of each other. I thought of the life we had created together and how we completed each other. The time apart seemed to make us realize that what we felt for each other was somehow seamlessly easy when we were by the other's side, but time apart flowed differently. Still, what we had apart was better than what most people would ever know in their lifetime. I sat and watched the fire, feeling it warm my body as it slowly burned down to small embers.

Then I slowly made my way out of the chair and toward the bedroom. I looked at the bed I shared with Keith and for a moment I thought of how hard it must be to climb into a bed so far away from home with nothing familiar around him. I climbed in to bed and hugged Keith's pillow. His scent was as strong as if he were truly there with me. I slowly fell asleep, thinking of how much our love meant to us, and how we had never tried to take advantage of our love for each other but treasured it for what it was, more precious than pure gold.

As the rising sun rays light the bedroom I rose quickly, hurrying through my morning routine before I went to the kitchen to start the coffee. During the wishing of a good day and exchange of love for each other, I could tell by Keith's voice he was longing to return home, but he was committed to the sculpture he was working on. He planned to get straight to sculpting in hopes of finishing quickly and making his way back home to me. We hung up and I sat and reflected on our wonderful life together for a moment longer.

Again, it seeming that every time I picked up the old handwritten correspondences my family sent to each other, it triggering the calling to the ocean's edge. The call was strong again this morning. I felt the need to make my way to the shore. Today the winds and the waves were calm, as if both had fallen asleep, like a ship's captain asleep at the helm, until I reached my usual spot. Then, out of nowhere the wind and the waves, like finely tuned instruments playing in unison, called to me. The voices of the past started to whisper in my ear and the stronger the waves and winds grew, the louder the voice called out, "My love, come to my side once more."

Again, heeding the voice I could hear fainting calling. Much to my surprise, I saw a little girl with two other children, another girl and a boy.

They were traveling in a covered wagon over a worn path. The father was talking to the children about their family's new beginning. He talked about the land, and the house, and the plans he had to build their life, and how happy they would be once they arrived. The woman was awfully quiet, and the kids didn't seem to be close to her. I heard the father explaining more about their new start for the whole family as he told the children, "You have a new mom now. Your mother passed. I want you children to call Fanny mama from now on."

The look in their eyes spoke of their love for their mother. They weren't ready for anyone else to take her place. But the children smiled at their father and said, "Yes, Papa." As they made their way closer to their new home. Papa told them they had one more stop to make. He explained he had asked their new neighbor, Mr. Tripp, to keep an eye on the place until he returned with the family. They would stop by and let him know they'd made it safely.

It wasn't long before they were at the Tripp's home. As we made our way up the drive we noticed Mr. Tripp had children, too. They seemed about our age, but my sister and I just dismissed the boys as someone for our brother, Daniel, to know. But when papa stopped the wagon and we all got off to stretch, I felt again the instant connection as two destined souls reconnected. At fifteen years-old, Rosepha and James met and their spirits seemed to communicate, as if catching up with each other, without a word being spoken between them. The parents made brief introductions and got their attention.

James stuck out his hand to Rosepha first and said, "Hello, I'm James."

"Hello, James, I'm Rosepha."

They were reluctant to release each other's hand. Mrs. Tripp noticed, but didn't say a word. She would not embarrass the two, but could already see the light shining deep within both the children. They did let go, when Daniel introduced himself and stuck his hand out to James. The introductions moved on to Martha and James's brother, Peleg, who was the age of my brother, Daniel. James and Rosepha were both 15 years of age. Daniel and Peleg were both 17, and Martha was 11.

Mr. Tripp said he would send the boys up to help unload the wagon and that he would send the boys up each day for a few days to help get things settled. My papa thanked Mr. and Mrs. Tripp for their kindness, and Mrs. Tripp gave mama a fresh baked loaf of bread as we made our way back to the wagon. James and Peleg climbed up into the wagon. James sat across from Rosepha and they stared into each other's eyes while her papa made the way up the road to their house. It was as if they were having a non-stop conversation without speaking a word. James and Peleg stayed and helped Papa and Daniel while Rosepha, Martha, and mama unpacked the skillets and plates and eating utensils. Mama made gravy to go with the bread and James and Daniel ate with us. Then papa told James and Peleg to jump back in the wagon so he would take them home before their parents started to worry. Papa and Daniel took them home and returned straight way, papa still had a few chores for him and Daniel before the day's light disappeared into the night sky. It had been a long day for everyone and when papa announced it was time for bed everyone was happy to hear it. Rosepha and Martha shared a bed. Martha was asleep as soon as her head hit the pillow, but Rosepha laid in bed for what seemed like hours, though it was only a few minutes, thinking of James and how she knew that when she grew up she wanted to marry him and be his wife for the rest of her life.

When James got home and finished his own chores, his mother called to him. Sitting alone on the porch with him she asked, "James, what do you think of the Comstock family?"

"Oh mama, they are great! I am so glad they moved here."

"James, what do you think of Rosepha?"

"Why, mama?" he asked, looking at her.

"I just was wondering what you thought of her."

"Do you really want to know what I think of her?"

"Yes, I do, James."

"Mama, one day I am going to marry Rosepha."

"You are?"

"Yes ma'am. She is going to be my wife and me her husband like you and Papa."

"You seem sure of that."

"Mama, I have no doubt about how we both feel. We are meant to be together."

"All right, then," his mother answered. "Now it's time for you to clean up and head to bed. You and your brother will be going to help Mr. Comstock and Daniel tomorrow. There's a lot of work to be done to help them get settled in."

James kissed his mother's cheek and went off as he'd been told. Mrs. Tripp sat on the porch for a little while, thinking back to the moment that morning when she saw her son and Rosepha met. The moment their eyes met had been magical, even if only she could see it. He has truly met his soulmate this morning, she thought.

It would be many years before their journey would turn to man and wife, but every choice they made from that day on would be with that one thought in mind. In just a moment, a twinkling of the eye, lives had been forever changed.

Mrs. Tripp had noticed that while Martha and her mama seemed close, Daniel and Rosepha didn't have the same relationship. Perhaps it had been the excitement of the day, but knowing Rosepha would one day be part of her family, she determined from that first day forward she would be treated that way. She was delighted to have the girl she had always wanted to teach to cook, to sew, to cross stitch, and to watch grow beautiful and confident. *I have one more child to watch over. I hope she will learn to think of me as family and to come to me with anything she needs.*

James was in his bed, tossing and turning, thinking of the future day when he and Rosepha would be together forever. He dozed off to sleep, thinking he couldn't wait to see her the next day.

The next morning came and Mrs. Tripp anticipated James wanting to get back up to the Comstock house as soon as possible, so she got up before dawn and started breakfast. She was right. James was up and dressed as the sun met the horizon. Peleg also got up early. He had a new friend in Daniel, Rosepha brother. James and Peleg went to the Comstock house for a few days and helped Mr. Comstock and Daniel, but they didn't see much of Mrs. Comstock or Daniel's sisters. They were inside helping their mama get the house in order. Still, Rosepha and James managed at least a few moments each day to see each other, to briefly feed their souls that thirsted for each other.

After the first few days, Peleg and James returned to their regular chores on their own farm. Not long after, Mrs. Tripp sent the boys up to the Comstock house to invite them to dinner. This gave James a chance to see Rosepha. She was all he kept on his mind now. They came back, James filled with excitement.

"They're coming to dinner, mama! I told them you said it would be at five." Mrs. Tripp sent the boys back out to do their chores and help their papa stacking wood.

"Tell your papa I said for all of you to clean up early before the Comstock's come."

Mrs. Tripp sat Rosepha across from James at the table. She knew they would want to be able to see each other, even if they didn't talk much, or at all. She sat Mrs. Comstock straight across from her so they could talk, with the same for Daniel and Peleg, and then the grown men. When the Comstock's arrived, Mrs. Tripp paid particular attention to how Mrs. Comstock interacted with Daniel, Rosepha, and Martha. When dinner was done, Rosepha helped Mrs. Tripp clean up while Mrs. Comstock sat with Martha by her side. After pie, when they were getting ready to go, Mrs. Tripp thanked Rosepha for her help and told Mrs. Comstock what a wonderful young lady Rosepha was, so very helpful. Mrs. Comstock hardly acknowledged the compliment. So Mrs. Tripp asked if she could send her husband up to fetch Rosepha the next day, to help her with her canning.

"I sure would love some help and I would be glad to send her home with some of the preserves for helping. First year harvest is always scant," said Mrs. Tripp. Mrs. Comstock agreed right away.

The next day, they'd only been in the kitchen a few minutes when Rosepha said, "She's not my mama."

"What?"

"Fanny's not my mama. My mama died last year and my papa married Fanny. He thought we should move and start a new life as a family in a new place. Fanny is kind enough, but she has only really taken to Martha. But that's ok, Daniel and I are pretty much grown and we don't want to replace our mother anyway."

"Oh, Rosepha," Mrs. Tripp said. "I'm so sorry to hear that. Well, I'd like you to think of this as home and us as your family, too. If you ever want to talk, you can come talk to me. I will always be here for you." Mrs. Tripp hugged Rosepha with a long motherly hug, the sort Rosepha had been missing since her mother died.

"I love my papa very much, and so do Daniel and Martha, but it is awkward for me and Daniel to accept Fanny. We're trying, for papa."

Three years had come and passed as Rosepha and Mrs. Tripp grew closer. She taught her how to cook, with the skill of a women instead of a child helping her mother, she taught her to darn socks to hold the mend for a man's foot. She taught her everything she had learned through her years as a wife and mother. She taught her the way she would have taught her own daughter if she had one. The morning of Rosepha's eighteenth birthday came and James knocked on the door of the Comstock's house.

Mr. Comstock answered, "Hello James, what can I do for you?"

"Mr. Comstock, I would like to ask for Rosepha's hand in marriage."

Mr. Comstock was shocked. "James, I didn't know you cared for Rosepha."

"Since the moment I met her, sir."

"Well, I like you a lot but I will have to ask Rosepha how she feels about all this first."

Mr. Comstock called Rosepha into the room and before he could ask she said, "Yes, Papa, I want to marry James."

"Well, all right. James, you heard Rosepha's answer, so I give you two my blessing. When is the big day going to be, James?"

"Well, sir, I have to go out of the state for as much as six months training as a military doctor and want to wait 'til I get back, but mama wanted to know if Rosepha could come and stay with her while I am gone. Peleg is in Virginia working since papa died. He has only been making it home on the weekends. She thought Rosepha would make great company for her while I was gone. Mama said Rosepha could have my room and could set it up anyway she liked. I thought it would be better to wait to marry when I got back. But I will marry her today if you would rather us be married before she goes to stay with my mama."

"James," Mr. Comstock chided, "We have known your family long enough to know you are good people. Yes, Rosepha can go stay with your mother while you're gone if she wants to."

Rosepha spoke up. "Oh, Papa, can I? Thank you! Yes, I would love to go stay with Mrs. Tripp."

Mr. Comstock asked, "What day you have to leave, James."

"Tomorrow, midday."

"After Rosepha gets packed, I will bring her down tomorrow morning so you two can spend some time together before you leave. We would all love to come down to see you off."

"Mama told me to invite you all down for a big early lunch tomorrow so we can visit before I take off."

"That sounds good, James. Tell your mother we'll be there. Now, if you two would like to go outside and visit and start making some plans, the front porch is free."

"Thank you, Mr. Comstock."

"Now, James," Mr. Comstock replied, "I insist you start calling me William."

"Ok, Mr. Comstock, I mean, William. I'll have to get used to that."

Rosepha and James walked out onto the front porch and James took Rosepha by the hand. "Rosepha, you know I have loved you from the moment I first saw you."

"And I you, James."

"I know we have never talked about love or much of anything since we've never had any time alone together. We were only able to talk to each other through our souls and through our eyes. I was hoping that everything I was saying, you were receiving."

"I was, everything James. I felt the same way. I hoped you were also always hearing what I was saying in return."

"I did, my love. The moment I saw you I felt as if I had always known you and that we were meant to be together the rest of our lives."

"You know I felt the same, James. Now in just a few short months we will be man and wife."

"How I have waited for this day. I would marry you before I leave, Rosepha, but I am afraid if I do, I won't be able to leave your side ever. I have a commitment I have to fulfill, so I think I should get it done first, and then we will not have anything standing in our way ever again."

"I understand. I don't think I could let you go once we were married either, so I think you made the right decision for us. With you away, I will be happier being at your house and sleeping in your room as close to you as I can be."

"It will still be hard to leave you tomorrow, but knowing you are with Mama will make it easier to bear for me. My mother already loves you as if you were her own. She is so excited that you will have each other for comfort while I am gone."

James sighed. "I don't want to leave you now, but there is much for me to do to get ready before I leave tomorrow to make it easier for you and my mother to get by. I also have to pack my bag. I want you to change my room to what you want it to be for the both of us. It will be the room we share to start our new life and it should reflect what makes you happy."

"Every time you talk about leaving, my spirit feels sadden by the thought of you being so far away from me, my sweet James."

"My love, it hurts my spirit, also. I tell you now, my love, we will be together, and when we become man and wife, together forever, nothing will ever part us again."

""'Til tomorrow then, my love. Have a wonderful day."

James kissed her for the first time, then jumped on his horse and left for home. Rosepha went back inside the house where her papa was waiting.

"My little girl has grown up right before my eyes and in a few short months she will marry the man of her dreams."

"Oh Papa, I do love him."

"I know, Rosepha. I have known since the day you met that this moment would come. I think everyone knew. Now go pack your things and spend a little time with your sister. She doesn't know yet. I thought I would leave that to you."

"Thank you, Papa." With a quick hug Rosepha was off to find her sister.

"Martha? Martha, guess what."

"What is it, Rosepha?"

"James and I are to be married! He just came and asked papa for my hand!"

"When will it be?"

Rosepha answered, "In a few months. James has to go away for a little bit and when he returns we are to be married right away. Help me pack, Martha, as we talk."

"But why are you packing now if you aren't marrying for few months?"

"I am going to stay with his mother 'til he gets back and then that's where we will live as man and wife."

"When are you going to stay with Mrs. Tripp?"

"Tomorrow."

"Tomorrow! I will miss you, Rosepha."

"You'll still see me, I'll ask papa to bring you to see me once a week when he goes into town. He can drop you off and pick you up on his way home."

"I don't want to lose you."

"Martha, I will be right down the road, and you are welcome to come see me anytime. You're my sister and always will be." Rosepha looked around. "Well, I've packed up most everything except my night clothes. Now, I have some laundry to wash."

"I'll help you with that."

Rosepha and Martha got the clothes washed and dried in the sun on the line, then ironed and folded. Then, it was time to make dinner and enjoy the last evening Rosepha would live in the house as part of the family.

The next morning, everyone rose early so they could spend a little more time together. Martha and mama made cinnamon rolls for a special goodbye. While they baked, Daniel and papa loaded my bags and hope chest into the wagon so nothing would be forgotten or left behind when it was time to leave. We sat down to eat the hot, fresh cinnamon rolls and my papa started to talk of my childhood and how fast I had grown before his eyes. Then he moved to James, and what a fine man he was and that he would make me a good husband. When the rolls were gone, Martha and Rosepha got up, cleared the table, and cleaned up the dishes. Papa and Daniel went out to finish up some chores before we made our way to James's house. I could feel Rosepha's heart pounding in anticipation of the start of a new chapter in her life as of the wife of James Tripp. Rosepha Tripp sounded exciting. She would finally be one with James, in spirit and body.

I could feel all of Rosepha's feelings as though they were my own, just as the other times. I thought we had been one together in spirit since the moment we met, but soon we would be complete. The morning I thought would drag on forever actually went fast. Soon all the chores were done and papa was coming in to say it was time to head out. I wanted to run and jump into the wagon like a school girl on her first day of school. Instead, I walked slowly with Martha. She was sad and wanted every moment she could with me before I left. I didn't want her to feel as if I didn't love her or wouldn't miss her. The ride we knew well to the Tripp's house seemed shorter than usual.

James and Mrs. Tripp came out on the porch to welcome us to their house. Daniel was the first off the wagon and helped mama down, then Martha. For the first time, James came over to help me down off the wagon. He showed Daniel and papa where to take my things. James's bags were already packed and waiting besides the front door. He had left all his personal things in his room for me. After everything was delivered and papa and Daniel had gone back out, James called me in for a private moment. He gave me a kiss and told me to do anything I wanted to the room to make it pleasing to his wife. As we stood there, the scent of James in his room overpowered my senses with comfort and love. It was as if, when I closed my eyes, his arms would be holding me in his. The thought brought a smile to my face and James knew the room pleased me. James told me he had put a letter in the top drawer of the dresser for me to read that night before bed, but not until then. I agreed to wait. Then Martha came in and handed me a small bag I left on the wagon.

"Oh, Rosepha, you have this big room to yourself?"

"For now she will," James answered with a grin. Then we all turned and walked downstairs to the living room where everyone was sitting. Papa and mama were talking to Mrs. Tripp.

Mrs. Tripp called me over to her. "Welcome to your new home."

I could see papa smiling as she told me that from now on I should call her Elizabeth. I agreed to try, but we all knew it would take a while. She smiled at me ever so sweetly as she held my hand in hers. Then Elizabeth announced that lunch was ready and turned to ask if I would help her serve. Oh yes, I was ready to be a part of this family. James looked at me and smiled, happy and proud to have me helping his mother serve guests in their home.

"Looks as if Rosepha will be right at home here with you," Papa commented. "It won't take her long before she knows where everything belongs."

"I'm looking forward to her company in the kitchen as I teach her to make all James's favorite foods."

After we had served everyone, Elizabeth and I sat at the table. She put James at the head of the table in his father's place and me at the other end in her usual spot so we could look at each other as much as we could before he left on his journey. Everyone talked to James about finishing up his degree in medicine and where he would be to do his internship in Alabama. He and papa talked about how long it would take to get there and the weather and what he could expect to be doing in his internship. Elizabeth and mama talked about the dessert and if Elizabeth would share the recipe. Martha had a quiet voice so I couldn't tell what she and Daniel were talking about at the other end of the table. Mostly, I kept looking at James and thinking how I would miss him. I hoped I would have a little time alone with him before he had to leave. James frequently looked into my eyes with longing as papa kept talking to him. Finally, lunch and dessert were done and the table cleared. Elizabeth suggested everyone say their goodbyes there and let James and I go out for a few private moments together before he left.

"I hadn't realized it was getting close to the time," Papa exclaimed. Everyone got up and headed to the door.

"I'll see you when you get back, James. Don't be gone any longer then you have to be." Daniel said, first to say his piece.

"No worries of that," James answered.

"Have a safe journey," Papa wished him. "And remember to write your mama and Rosepha often. If you need anything from me or Daniel, for any reason, you get a hold of us."

"I'll do that, William." James assured him.

Mama and Martha were brief, just wishing him a safe journey. Then they loaded up in the wagon and headed back to their farm as we waved goodbye. It felt odd to not think of it as home, but I was already home, where I'd always wanted to be, at James's side.

Elizabeth turned to the young couple and said, "Son, it is getting close to the time you have to leave. I will go in and make you a pouch of leftovers and dessert for you to eat along the way while you and Rosepha have some time to yourselves." Then Elizabeth turned and went inside, closing the door behind her.

James took my hand in his and said, "Rosepha, I wish we had longer to spend alone together before I leave, but the time is short. I will miss you terribly, my love. I wish I didn't have to leave you for a moment, but I promise this will be the only time I will leave you in our lifetime. After this we will be together forever as man and wife and we will not be parted from each other until death."

"How I will miss you, James, but I am so glad I will be here with your mother and in your room."

"Our room, my love. Anything that is mine is now yours from now to death. My mind will be so much more at ease knowing you and my mother will be here, together, in the home where we will start our lives together. Come closer, let me hold you in my arms and kiss your sweet lips before I leave. Remember my love, when I return you will become my wife. You are my present and my future. I will think of you every day with tender love and I will dream of you each night until I return. I will write you each and every day." He paused, then asked, "Rosepha, may I have something of yours? A kerchief? Anything that belongs to you to carry with me."

Rosepha turned. "Yes, of course. Let me go and get a clean one out of my trunk."

James lightly took her arm to stop her racing off. "My love, could I have the one you have on? It has your scent on it and that is what I want, my love, to be able to smell your scent. When I close my eyes at night it will bring me home to you in my thoughts and dreams, as if I was back here by your side.

I slowly took the one from around my neck and placed it around James's neck as he leaned down for me to reach. Then he took me into his arms again.

"My time is running out. I need to go say goodbye to my mother before I leave." With that we separated and he went to the door to call for his mother. As he reached inside and grabbed his bag, he called, "Mama! Time to go, come say goodbye!"

Elizabeth rushed to the porch and joined us there. James already had the saddle and packs on his horse, everything but the bag of food Elizabeth had made and was holding for him as he hugged and kissed her upon her forehead. With one more kiss for me on my lips, he mounted his horse and took the food bag from Elizabeth.

"You two ladies take care of each other while I am gone. I will be back before you know it." Then he turned his horses and took off before we could say another word.

Then Elizabeth turned to me. "The time will fly by, Rosepha, just you wait and see."

I said, "I sure hope you're right."

"Come sit with me on the porch swing for a little while. In a bit we will go and eat some leftovers and then you can go to your room and put away your things. Do you want help? I always like to do it myself, but I'd love to help if you want."

"I think I would like to do it myself."

We sat and talked for an hour, her trying to ease my mind, assuring me that time would fly by. After which we went inside to eat and plan what we should do the next day. After we ate, I went upstairs and started down the hall to my room. The closer I got to my room the more I could smell James's scent, stronger with each step. Oh the warmth I felt from just his scent. It was so comforting to me. I was glad to be there, with his scent and his things, rather than back at my papa's house. I was ready for him to be a part of my life from now on, even if it was only his things and his room. I opened the door to our bedroom. His scent was as strong as it had been when I was in his arms on the porch. I closed my eyes and drew it in deeply. Then I opened my eyes and grabbed my first bag, feeling his presence in the room. I opened the first dresser drawer to put my clothes in and saw the note James had left for me, laying on top of one of his night shirts. It wasn't yet bed time, but I wanted to see what he had said. Maybe he had wanted me to leave this drawer for him.

My love, by now I have gone and you are starting to unpack. I left this nightshirt of mine for you. I thought you might like to wear it to sleep. You can smell my scent and dream of me holding you closely in my arms as you rest your head upon your pillow on our bed, tonight and every night until I

return and make you my bride.

I set the nightshirt on the bed along with the letter as I started emptying my trunks and putting my things about me. I felt very comfortable in this room. There was nothing to adjust to, no slow getting accustomed, this was my home. For the first time, I know I am where I belong. My trunk finally emptied, and I had put away the things in my hope chest. Some of those had been my mother's, locked away since I was little girl. I hadn't dared to take them out to admire, it would have caused problems with Fanny. I could remember to call Fanny mama in front of papa, but in my thoughts, I called her Fanny. I had missed my mama for so long. I always felt like I couldn't mourn or talk about her in front of Papa and Fanny since Papa wanted us to accept

Fanny as our mama. As if it were that easy. It's not that Fanny wasn't kind to us, and Martha and Fanny became very close, but for me and Daniel—we were older and closer to our own mother. Fanny just didn't take to Daniel or me like she did Martha. She didn't even try. I had felt closer to James's whole family from the first meeting. Elizabeth had taken me under her wing. She got papa to let me come help her with her women's work whenever she had a chance. I already loved Elizabeth and she was the nearest thing I felt I had to a mother.

That night I retired to our room that smelled so wonderfully of James. I wasn't sure if it would be easy or hard to fall asleep with his sent so strong. I walked to my new dresser and pulled out James's night shirt. It felt natural on my body, as if I'd already worn it many times. I thought of all the times this shirt had covered James's body and it almost felt as if his flesh was touching mine. I wondered if it would affect my dreams. I was tired from the long day, between the families gathering, saying goodbye to the ones who had always been my family, and then to say goodbye to the love of my life who would be my family going forward. I was ready for a good night's sleep. It seemed very strange to climb into James's bed, knowing that one day soon we would share it as husband and wife. I pulled the covers up high and hugged the pillow to me as if it were James. I closed my eyes and took a deep breath to get as much of his scent as I could and I was asleep in a moment.

The next day the morning light made its way into the room to welcome me to a new day in my new room and new life. I jumped to my feet and dressed, then made my way down to the kitchen to wish good morning to Elizabeth. Elizabeth had started the fire to make coffee and cook biscuits for breakfast. She turned when she heard me.

"Good morning! I hope you slept well."

"Oh, yes, ma'am. I slept very well, thank you."

"Coffee?"

She turned with a big smile. "You feel as though this is your home already, don't you Rosepha?"

"Yes, I do. How did you know?"

"Just the way you come into the room. The look on your face was very peaceful with a gentle smile."

"Oh Elizabeth, you've always made me feel so welcome, It's as if this has always been home. I am very comfortable here, but I miss James something horrible."

"I know," Elizabeth comforted. "But we must keep our minds and hands busy. It will make the time pass quicker."

"I know," Rosepha replied, "But at moments like this, it's really hard."

The morning passed quickly as they drank coffee and made biscuits. They ate and did the rest of their women's chores. I pitched right in to help Elizabeth with all her chores, inside and out. The day was closing quickly when they both realized they hadn't had lunch and it was already time for dinner. They retreated back into the kitchen to cut some ham and bread from a loaf that Elizabeth had made the day before, deciding on cold sandwiches for the evening meal. They planned to bake bread for the week the next day, and discussed a fun dessert. To make a full day of cooking they decided to add in a fresh pot of soup. Elizabeth didn't mention it, but she thought it was a good idea to keep Rosepha too busy to pine for her son. Pining would make the time pass too slowly.

Just being in James's house and among his things, and now mine combined with his, gave me a peace inside that I had never found in the house that up until now I had called home. I longed for the day that James would come home, but until then I busied myself making things for the house with his mother. I did a cross stitch for our wedding, everything finished but the date.

One evening as I finished my stitching, I ask Elizabeth, "What were your parents like?"

She paused from her reading and looked at me. "Well, they were kind, hardworking people."

"Where were you raised? How was your life?"

"Why the questions?"

"I want to start a journal about both sides of our new families. Someday I will be a mother and I wanted to be able to tell them about their history. It seemed like a good, ambitious project to keep me and you occupied while James was away," I said, looking down at my needlework.

"I think that is a splendid idea, Rosepha," Elizabeth said as she stood. "Let's go into the living room where we can sit and talk about our ancestors."

I took pen in hand to write as she talked and I asked questions. The time passed quickly. Before we knew it we were both tired and ready for bed. We said our goodnights and headed to our rooms. I was pleased how well the days kept me busy, but James stayed close in my thoughts and heart. I decided the next day I would write a letter to him. Papa told me he would look for letters at the post office in town and if I had one to send, he'd take it for me or Elizabeth. I was hoping to get a letter from James, letting us know he'd made it to his destination. As always, I again put on the night shirt James had left me and climbed into bed. I fell asleep thinking about him. The next thought I had was of the strong morning light that flowed into the windows. I made my way out of bed and dressed before heading down the stairs to the kitchen. Elizabeth had already made the coffee and started the biscuits.

That evening at supper I said, "I'm going to write a letter to James. If you want to write, too, we can put it in the same envelop. My papa will collect it in the morning on his way to town."

"I think I will. That's a great idea. He will love hearing how we are managing together."

It became a comforting routine for me to write James every night after dinner. Then once a week Elizabeth would write him, also. Their other favorite evening activity was sharing their ancestry. They would go into the living room and Elizabeth would tell her of what she knew of the Tripp family, and about her own family and ancestors. Before either knew, two months had gone by and they were far behind on their stitching plans. They hadn't even started on the needle point bedcover Rosepha had planned to make for her marriage bed.

Peleg was due for a visit soon so the women cleaned his room and laundered the sheets. Elizabeth was very excited. Peleg had been gone for three months. She'd gotten letters, but it wasn't the same. Until she could see his face, she couldn't be sure he was really okay. They spent a few days before he arrived preparing some of his favorite foods and desserts.

The day he was due to arrive, Elizabeth could barely stay off the porch for watching for him. As early evening approached, so did Peleg.

Elizabeth was smiling from ear to ear as he climbed down from his horse and made his way to the porch with a big hug and kiss upon the forehead for his mother.

He turned and asked, "So, are you and James married yet?"

I answered with a smile. "Soon, but not yet."

"Where is James, still in Alabama?"

"He is. It will be a few more months."

"You're staying here to take care of our mama while he's away?"

She laughed. "I don't know who is taking care of who, but yes, I am staying here."

"I guess you're here to stay then, since you will be marrying him when he gets back."

Elizabeth chimed in, smiling. "That's right, Peleg. Rosepha is ours for good now."

I tried to give Peleg and Elizabeth some mother-son time, but they both pulled me into the conversations as part of the family. I truly did feel as if I belonged in every aspect. I worried at first that the scent of Peleg in the house would wash away the scent of James, but James's scent was the only one I ever picked up in the house. To me it was like a strong perfume, strong even in his many times laundered night shirt.

The next day my brother and Martha came for the day. Peleg and Daniel hadn't seen each other for a while and wanted to catch up, so instead of papa bringing Martha this week, it was Daniel. They came early and stayed the whole day, even for supper, before going back home. Peleg planned to leave the following day.

Daniel handed me a letter from James. As with all the many letters he had sent, he started out with, my love, my life, always how I miss you and long for my return home to you. Most of the rest I could read out loud to let Elizabeth and Peleg, and today Daniel and Martha, know how he was doing and that all was well with him. It was going on over four months since I last saw James, and my longing for him grew stronger every day.

The next morning, I woke before anyone else and made my way down to the kitchen. I wanted to make coffee and breakfast for Elizabeth and Peleg so they would have more time to visit before he left. I cleaned the kitchen after so they could go out onto the porch and swing and visit and talk before he had to go. After I finished up the chores, I joined them on the porch but he soon stood and announced it was time to go. I grabbed the pouch of food I had made for his trip and handed it to Elizabeth to give him. I wished him well and he shared with me how glad he was that James and I would finally be married soon and how nice it was that I had already moved in and was there with his mother. I could tell that Elizabeth didn't want him leave, as if she thought it was the last time she would see him, but as Peleg rode off she returned to her normal self.

Every day was filled with something for us to do. It kept us occupied until there was only one more week until James would return. I thought everything was perfect with nothing to worry about when papa showed up with a letter from someone in Virginia. Peleg was missing and presumed dead. I thought Elizabeth was going to faint. Papa and I helped her to a chair. He told Elizabeth that he would tell Daniel and when James returned he could join us in the search. That is if we haven't already return home by then. From that moment the remaining days until James returned passed ever so slowly, but the day did come. James arrived home early in the morning but didn't come alone. He had a preacher with him. By the time I could get out the door he was already off his horse and making his way to draw me into his arms. Elizabeth came out to see the preacher getting off his horse.

"I guess you plan to marry this morning, James." Elizabeth laughed.

"Yes, Mama, if Rosepha is still willing to marry me, this morning."

I started to respond with joy only to think of Peleg. James didn't know Peleg was missing and thought dead. "James, let me talk with your mama a moment before we get married." He looked puzzled but agreed.

"We should put this off until they find Peleg."

"Absolutely not," Elizabeth argued. "I want you two to be married before James goes anywhere. Don't say a word. I will tell him tomorrow morning."

"But..."

"Rosepha, I mean it. I will tell him tomorrow."

So Rosepha walked back over to James's side and as James took Rosepha's hand in his, he said, "I can tell by the look in your eyes we are still as one, so is everything else ok?"

Rosepha smiled. "I am ready to become your wife and your bride."

With that James called out to the preacher, "We are ready to get married!"

The preacher married them and they went off together to be alone for a while. James took Rosepha down to the river that ran through the property. He laid her down on his coat and kissed her sweet, gentle lips. He would wait to make love to her in their bed at home if she wanted. He said, or they could there on the riverside.

"James, make love to me now. Don't make me wait another minute to feel you inside of me."

James lifted Rosepha's dress as he slipped himself inside her. They were both lost in the moment as their bodies became one as their souls had been for many years. They lay together for an hour before they stood up from the ground and meandered back to the house, hand in hand. They stopped every few moments to kiss and look into each other's eyes. The love their souls held for each other beamed ever so brightly.

As they approach the house, Rosepha took James by the arm to get his attention and said, "James, your mother has something to tell you. She said she wanted to wait until morning but I think she should tell you tonight."

"What is it?"

"I promised your mother I would not to tell you. It is her place to explain and in her time. But I think you could convince her to tell you tonight, if you tried."

As they walked up to the house, there sat Elizabeth with a look of sadness mingled with happiness.

"Mama, Rosepha said there is something you need to tell me in the morning, but she thinks you should tell me tonight."

"I didn't want to ruin your wedding day," Elizabeth said sadly.

"Mama, you have to tell me what it is tonight."

"If you insist. We got word, a little less than a week ago, after you had already left to come back that Peleg was missing and presumed dead. Daniel and William already left to go looking for him to bring him back home, alive or dead. Daniel gave me this letter to let you know where you could find the place they would be looking, so you could join in the search if they hadn't returned before you got home."

"Oh, Mama! I am so sorry."

"I know, son, and I didn't want to make you and Rosepha wait until to you got back again. It wouldn't be fair to either one of you."

"I'll plan to leave in the morning." He took the letter from his mother.

"This is your wedding day. You should be spending time with your bride."

"Rosepha and I have the rest of our lives together, but you need me now and Rosepha knows that."

I added, "Elizabeth, this is what we need to do for you right now. Our love is strong and we will be fine. James needs to find out what happened to Peleg, for all of us. So please quit worrying about it being our wedding day. We are equally concerned and want nothing more than to find out the truth. It doesn't take away from this day for us. We love and draw closer to each other when we face trouble. It shows us the strength we hold within ourselves and together we learn to manage the hardship and sacrifice we will have to endure through our lives as a couple."

Elizabeth smiled and hugged me. "I would never have managed all these months with James and Peleg gone without you here with me. You have given me strength."

James finished Daniel's letter. He announced that he would leave to join them at mornings light. The day passed in a busy haze and it was now supper-time. I cooked as I talked to Elizabeth, sitting at the kitchen table. James was hungry but hadn't until that moment realized he hadn't eat since yesterday. He wanted to get home early in the morning and had gotten up before dawn. I fixed him a large plate of food, but Elizabeth could eat little, worrying about Peleg. After we ate,

James and Elizabeth talked at the table while I cleared it and did the dishes. Then I made James a pouch of food to take in the morning so he could eat on his way, and I put extra in it for Daniel and Papa, too. Then I joined them, but we moved to the living room to sit in more comfortable chairs.

We sat and talked to Elizabeth for a few hours before Elizabeth announced, "I am worn out. I think I will go to bed. James, if I don't see you in the morning before you leave, have a safe journey. Now give your mama a hug so I can go to bed."

James got up and gave his mother a strong, yet, gentle hug. Then off to bed she went. James turned and looked into my eyes as he walked over to me and took hold of my hand, pulling me up from the chair and into his arms. "What a mess. I am so sorry, Rosepha. This is our wedding day and we have had very little time to spend alone together. Now, I have to wake early and leave you yet again even though I promised you when I returned I wouldn't leave you again."

"James, my love, I understand, and I am ok with it. Please don't feel bad. You will return to me again as soon as you can. I have no doubt."

"Come to our bed and lay with me before morning comes and I have to leave."

We made their way up the stairs. As I had done since moving in to the Tripp home, I took a deep breath to smell his scent, making my way down the hall. As James opened the door to our bedroom he gently put his arm low around my back and lifted me into his arms. He carried me into the room and laid me upon the bed. James laid down beside me and started kissing my lips and fondling my whole body, as if not to miss as single spot. It was as if he was trying to burn my shape into his memory, to hold me close while he was gone. He closed his eyes visualizing, every inch. Then he slowly undressed me and then himself and laid on top of me. He thrust himself into me without a word being spoken. Their bodies entwined and wrapped around each other as if fused together. It was hours before their bodies released from each other and they laid in each other's arms through the night, not speaking, not breaking the spell cast by the union of their bodies joining together. James fell asleep while starring into Rosepha eyes and she fell asleep moments later. They had spent most of the night awake and making love to each other. In the morning, James tried to get out of bed without waking her, but realized he couldn't leave without kissing her and telling her how much he loved her. It didn't matter. As soon as James started to move one arm she woke and smiled at him.

"I have to go. Kiss me and hold me as though it will last forever." When eventually she relaxed her arms, he said, "I will be home as soon as I am able. Let me leave seeing you laying upon our bed with the love in your eyes lighting the room."

Then he kissed me one last time, turned and left. I jumped to the floor to look out the window. I heard James getting onto his horse, and they rode off.

I dressed and went down to the kitchen to make coffee and breakfast. When Elizabeth appeared in the kitchen she asked, "What time did James head out this morning?"

"Just a little while ago."

Then the two sat to have breakfast and went into their normal routine for the day. They didn't speak much of James. They both knew why he had left. The day crept by and finally it was time for bed. Rosepha went to the bedroom that now belonged to her and James as man and wife. She didn't want to climb into the bed again without James, but forced herself anyway. She laid there for a while before falling asleep, reliving the night before, lying there and making love to James. It was like a dream to her, alone in the bed again. I have never made love to anyone before, so it must be real, she thought, it was real. She slowly drifted to sleep, holding James's pillows in her arms as she did when he had been gone those six months.

Morning came with dark gray clouds blanketing the sky, and without the light of sun shining in upon her face and waking her. Rosepha having woke late hurried to dress and make her way to the kitchen. But paused for a moment and thought to herself how she enjoyed it more on sunny mornings as if James had somehow sent the sun to kiss her good morning. She expected James would be gone a few days to a week finding out all the details. If Peleg had actually died they'd have to find out where his body was and arrange to bring it home to bury him in the family plot. She made her way to the kitchen and found Elizabeth had beat her down, coffee and breakfast were already waiting.

The days crawled by with little talk of James and the mission he was on until the day finally came that Daniel and James rode up. They left their horses unhitched as they came into the kitchen to tell Elizabeth the story of what had happened. Peleg was indeed dead, and his remains were impossible to recover. There had been an explosion at the coal mine where he worked. His mother accepted the facts as truth coming from James. Rosepha listened as she prepared food for James and Daniel. When they finished talking, James came over to her where she was cooking and whispered in her ear, "I missed you my love, and I am happy to be back home with you again."

Rosepha blushed. "Go sit down at the table. The food is ready."

James turned and sat down with a big smile upon his face. Despite the sad news they had brought, Elizabeth and Daniel were pleased to see James smiling. He was reunited with his bride and he was in love. When he finished eating, Daniel went home and Elizabeth got up and started busying herself in the kitchen. She sent James and Rosepha out to the porch to catch up with each other. They sat on the porch all day. It gave Elizabeth some time to herself to accept that her worst fear had come true. Peleg was gone.

Finally, together as they had wished, the newlyweds enjoyed just having time to be together as man and wife. Neither were much for talking, for years they had been able to read every thought the other had from watching their face. The days and months flew by after James was home. Rosepha and

James had two children, boys. Elizabeth loved having grandchildren.

James grew restless as a doctor and wanted to try his hand at something else. He wanted to move to the coast and open a store. They sold off everything that wouldn't fit in the wagon, including the farm. With a large sum of money, they took off to the coast. Elizabeth came with them and helped Rosepha with the boys. They built a store and a house down on the edge of Whitewater. They soon adapted to their new surroundings and were as happy as ever in their new life.

Then one day, Rosepha started getting a strange and uncomfortable feeling. She felt heavy, as if something was coming. She stayed as close to James's side as possible. Until one day, two neighbors came running into the store calling for James to come and help. There was a young Indian boy on the outskirts of town, lying on the side of the road. He needed help and the town doctor was delivering a baby. James grabbed his old medical bag and went to see what he could do to help. They made their way to where the boy laid on the road. James failed to use caution in his rush to climb down off the buggy, causing him to trip on a rock and hit his head. He died instantly. The other men put James in the wagon and headed back to town. Now there were two dead, and someone would have to tell Rosepha the news.

As they rode into town with James in the back of the buckboard, the wind blew up so strong that mist from the ocean splashed my face and brought me back to the present. I was sitting at the ocean's edge on a rock, half frozen from the winter wind. I jumped up from the rock and ran for home. The fire I had started in the fireplace that morning had dwindled to ash with only a few embers glowing. I coaxed it back to a flame with some fresh kindling and a small log and then headed to the shower to get warm. The hot water felt good on my body as it warmed me. I stood directly under the shower head, greedy to get every hot drop onto my body. Warm at last, I headed to the living room in my thick robe and toasty slippers. I made a small pot of coffee and checked my laptop to see if Keith had called yet. Nothing. Soon, I thought.

Sure enough, my can of soup wasn't even heated when the computer started to ring. In that moment it hit me what a wonderful and fulfilling life I had with Keith. Since the moment I'd met him it had been wonderful. No second guessing, never thinking for a moment what life would be like without him. For a moment, I tried to force myself to imagine life without him and my mind wouldn't even go there. I never gave another man a second thought in all the 17 years we'd been together, not even in a fantasy. I knew with every ounce of my being there could be no other man for me. It made me feel sad for those wandering the earth, forever searching in vain for their soulmates. Did they give up too soon and settle for second best? I couldn't imagine that the soul ever gave up looking, reaching for the one they instinctively knew was a match, out there somewhere. I think sometimes people didn't even realize how they would scan everyone they met for someone their soul hungers for, but hasn't found yet. My heavy thoughts had only taken seconds, the computer still ringing. I looked into Keith's eyes, and even through this distant connection my soul still leapt in excitement at the sound of his voice and the look in his eyes. My soul feels refilled.

"The sculpture is almost finished. I'll be coming home soon," he said on a sigh.

"That is wonderful. I have missed you terribly."

"Have you had any more callings to the ocean's edge?" Concern filled his voice, making it sound thick.

"Yes, today. It was incredibly real. I will tell you all about it when you get home."

"Should I be concerned?"

"No, I do not believe I am in danger. I believe I am being gifted with seeing our past lives."

"Ok, then. Better your experiences and the excitement of my project at its final stages of completion, we have much to be thankful for."

"Yes, we do. I am almost done with the ancestry research for the *Mayflower* proof and I will be getting it off in the mail soon."

"That is wonderful."

"I miss you so much."

"I miss you, too. It has been a long day though and I am afraid I will fall asleep while Skyping with you. I should hang up, my love."

"All right. I love you." The screen flickered and I could feel his soul.

"I love you, too." He yawned, but his eyes sparkled.

We hung up and I went back to the living room with the fire and started to go through the documents I had gathered over of the last six months. I checked to make sure I had them in order of generation, births and marriages. When I saw one small stack separated from the rest, I remembered I had set them aside to read about one of my grandmothers from a century ago. I picked them up and started to read about the life of Clara. Some of the pages were firsthand accounts handed down through family members and some were stories told by a daughter, and then a granddaughter of Clara.

The pages were worn and they grew heavy in my hands. I set them down.

Chapter Eight

Later that evening, when I felt I could live another life, I picked up the worn pages and began. Clara lived in the middle of the nineteen century. Her parents were well-off. They owned a canning business started by her grandfather. She wanted for nothing and was, from what I gather, beautiful to look at and quite the socialite. Her parents threw big parties for her and invited all of the who's who in their town. Her father was big into the politics, too, and he often invited many of the up and coming politicians to their home. One day her father came home with a strong, tall, good looking man he had asked over for dinner. Clara wasn't home when they arrived, she had been out shopping with her sister in preparation for a ball they would attend the next week.

When they arrived, they sought out their parents with excitement to show them what they had bought. When they got to the living room, there sat Clara's father and William. William immediately jumped to his feet when the two young women entered the room. Their father, Thomas, introduced William to his two daughters. It was apparent to everyone in the room that Clara and William connected right away. Clara, usually the most outgoing and talkative of the sisters, was at a loss for words. All Clara could do was to stare into Williams eyes. It seemed to everyone in the room that everything the two had to say was being said to each other without words. Even though it was early evening and the sun had mostly set, it seemed as though the room was brightly shining. Their mother entered from the kitchen to announce that dinner was ready and invited them all to the dining room. Clara's father tried talking to William on the way into the dining room, but it was hopeless, William and Clara were in a world of their own.

Her father gave up his plans to talk of politics for the rest of the evening. He wasn't too disappointed. This was the first time he had ever seen his daughter so quiet and drawn to a man. He thought Clara had finally found love. This was the man she would marry and spend the rest of her life with. Her sister and mother knew it, also. The connection was obvious. So her father kept the conversation light and only asked easy to answer questions. He now wanted to know more about the man than just his political ambitions. He wanted to know where he came from. Who his parents were. What his short term and long term goals were—all the questions a father would want to know about his future son-in-law. This wasn't what he had expected from his dinner invitation, but he wasn't unhappy about it. He had been talking politics with William for weeks now and liked what he had to say and how he expressed himself on the subject.

Memories of Clara growing up seem to take over the thoughts of her parents. Clara's father and mother knew they would be losing their little girl to this man soon. The dinner table conversation shifted to talk about Clara and her childhood and continued as they made their way back to the living room. William was very interested. Clara didn't mind that they were sharing all her childhood stories and secrets. The evening went quickly before Clara's sister excused herself.

Thomas stood. "I didn't realize how late it is. We must all be getting to bed soon, it will be an early day tomorrow."

"I'm sorry, I didn't mean to take up your family's whole evening," William said.

Thomas laughed. "We enjoyed your company. I'm sure we will be seeing a lot of you around here."

They walked to the door while Clara and her mother sat in the living room. When they reached the door, William asked, "Thomas, may I ask your permission to ask your daughter, Clara out for an evening soon?"

"It's fine with me, but you will have to ask Clara if she would like to go out with you." He called Clara to the front door. "William has something to ask you, Clara. I'll leave you two here for a moment alone."

Now, William had to vocalize the thoughts that he had been expressing through his eyes and soul all night. "Clara," William asked, "Would you like to go to the park tomorrow for a rowboat ride on the lake?"

Clara lit up. "Oh, yes, William, I would love to."

"What time shall I call for you?"

They agreed that ten in the morning would be best, and Clara would have a picnic lunch made up for them to eat. Thomas came back to the door and asked if they had made their plans. They agreed they had, so Thomas reminded both of them how late it was getting. William said goodnight again to Clara and Thomas and turned for the door.

Clara looked at her father, lost in thought, and he said, "Don't worry, you will see him tomorrow, my Clara."

Thomas knew that he wouldn't get to call her his Clara much longer. She kissed him goodnight and went to her room. As she climbed into the bed, she realized she already felt lost without William's presence in the same room with her. She realized that even if he were to ask her to marry the next day, it would be at least six months before that could take place. The social status of her family and proper etiquette wouldn't allow for any sooner. She knew there was no way her father and mother would agree to any other kind of wedding. She couldn't stand the thought, and she definitely couldn't imagine a long engagement. She wanted to be William's wife. She didn't want to wait. She didn't even like that he had left her side, and they weren't even married yet. Her thoughts kept running as she fell asleep.

The next morning, she awoke and wondered if everything had been a dream until there was a knock on her door. Her sister came in talking about William and how excited she was for her. Then Clara knew it was real. She told her sister, Virginia, of her plans as they hurried downstairs. They made their way to the dining room and before sitting down to breakfast, Clara asked her mother to have the cook make a picnic lunch for her and William.

"I already did," her mother assured her. "I heard you ask him if he would like you to bring one."

"Oh, thank you, mother."

"Your father said you can bring him home for dinner again if you would like."

Clara thought at that moment it was the closest thing to Heaven she could imagine. William would be there to pick her up soon and she would have an entire day and evening with him. Clara waited by the door with picnic basket in hand for his arrival. She opened the door and called her goodbyes back into the house as she was walking out and closed the door behind her. William helped Clara into his buggy and off they went to the lake.

It was a beautiful day with a lot of people out boating. They got into a boat and William rowed them out far from shore where they would be by themselves. The lake was crowded with other boats, but they mostly stayed close to the shore. William wanted privacy to ask her a question, but he wasn't sure he knew what her answer would be, so he did what he could to have privacy in a socially acceptable way.

"Clara, I know we just met, but I feel as if I have known you a lifetime. I cannot imagine my life from this point on without you, and if your father agrees, I want you to be my wife."

"I know. I love you and I know I always will. I don't want to be away from you any longer than I have to from now on, my love. I want nothing more than to be your wife as soon as possible."

They gazed at each other intently. William asked, "Clara, may I give you a kiss?" Clara nodded. They carefully drew close to each other so they would not tip the boat and William kissed her. "Do you think your parents will agree?"

Clara answered, "I think they will say, yes, but they will make us wait at least six months before they will allow it. Mother will have to get announcements out and parties will have to be thrown for us and bridal showers and all the wedding details. I felt lost without you after you left last night, but we'll have to wait."

"I missed you, too, my love. As I laid my head on my pillow, I already missed your presence around me. I feel your energy when you are near me. It feels as if I have been reborn. But my parents are the same and they'll be having parties for us, too. I just wish it didn't have to be so long before you could be my wife."

Clara and William spent the day together rowing around the lake and enjoyed their picnic at the park. They felt as if they had nothing or nowhere else to be or do, as if they were the only two people on earth. In that time and space nothing else existed. They stayed at the park until the evening light was fading into darkness. They left arm in arm, William helping her up into the buggy to make their way back Clara's house. They hurried inside, knowing that the family would be getting ready to sit down to dinner.

They were barely seated before Clara's mother asked about their day. "How was the lake? Did you enjoy your picnic?"

Clara glowed. "The day was great and the blue sky was beautiful and the sun was warm for a mid-spring day."

"And what did you talk about?"

"We talked a lot about family and social graces."

"That is a nice topic of conversation."

Virginia asked, "Did you run in to anyone we know?"

Clara thought for a moment. If there had been others around, she had blocked them out. It seemed to her as if she and William had been alone on a desert island. "No, Virginia, I didn't see anyone we know there today."

Her father asked, "William, how was the rowing?"

"Pleasant, thank you."

"Were the fish jumping?"

William stared at him a moment and then said, "I didn't notice."

That caused a big smile to cross Thomas's face. Clara was confused by the reaction. Not wanting to embarrass William, Thomas didn't mention that William was an avid fisherman and the two often discussed fishing.

William and Clara had talked on the way back to her house from the lake about when

William would approach her father about her hand in marriage. They decided right after the family dinner would be best. Clara suggested he draw Thomas out onto the porch for a cigar and talk.

But, Clara's family could tell they had already talked about marriage, so while everyone was still sitting at the table he announced, "The answer to that question you're planning to ask me later is, yes, William, you may marry our Clara." Clara and William shared a look of relief and excitement. Thomas grinned. "I thought I would just go ahead and get that out of the way so the women can get this all planned out. The quicker we start the planning, the faster you two can get married and we can all tell you two don't want to wait any longer than you have to. But you will have to wait six months before you say I do."

"We know, Papa."

Then Clara's mother said, "William, you will have to give me your mother's address so we can invite them over to have dinner with us, and get acquainted. She'll want to help with the planning and give us her guest list. I suggest you tell your parents tomorrow of your plans. Let your mother know that I will call on her her in a few days."

William smiled. "Yes, ma'am. I will."

I could tell by the reading of the papers that the family drew William in close. Thomas made William a partner in the family business and William and Clara built their home close to her parents' house. They named two of their children after her mother and father. Her sister married someone from out of state and moved away, she only visited occasionally. The papers I held in my hands went on as if it were a book just about her life. I could tell by reading that they loved each other from the moment they met to the moment of their deaths. They were forever entwined in their love, and they spent every moment of their lives together that they possibly could. They even promised to find and love each other in the future, as long as their spirits existed, no matter who they became in life.

They would be forever connected and time could not bind their love to just one lifetime. I wished I could have met them. Then I thought, Keith and I could be them living other lives. Transformed into new bodies with old souls that walked and loved in their lifetime and now this one. Even the past lifetimes I had glimpsed in the days I had spent at ocean's edge, those many weeks that Keith has been in Canada, might be the same souls. The treasured family records, documents, letters, and books that I had read of my family brought them back to life in my thoughts and dreams. I looked for one more document or paper that would give me more insight into the lives they had led. Each piece of paper was like a piece of a puzzle, fitting the past together just a bit more. It reminded me of a storyteller with an ending they somehow needed to build for the story to fit. With every little bit more information I found and treasured, I still wondered about all the pieces lost from the generations who assumed the story of their day to day lives would be unimportant to those in generations to come. I was so drawn to the past, it felt as if I were looking back at past lives I had lived. I felt as if I walked in their footsteps without missing a step.

How can anyone know that other people are in love just by looking at them? If the eyes are the windows to our souls, can you tell if the two souls are connected spiritually? Wasn't it possible they had met in another life because they felt in that first instant of meeting that they had known each other since their souls came into existence? With two souls creating such a positive energy that is constantly giving each other more energy resulting in an endless energy, never taking from each other or feeding off the other's life energy, as we see so many people in this world do, like robbery. Or, we see people who constantly give all their life energy to anyone who wants it, leaving themselves drained and too exhausted to have anything left to give at the end of their life. Always hoping someone along the way will want to give and share equally the energy burning within them. To feel love and comfort in life with the sharing from one to another soul in a true connection of their life's path on earth. How wonderful and enlightened it is when two souls meet and know it in that moment without any doubt or reservations that their life on earth is now complete, from that moment to the last breath that their bodies will take will be with that one person. They know they will not move any further in time without that person beside them, building and adding to the others' life energy. I can't even begin to remember anymore what life was like without my soulmate by my side, with me, in me, always there to give me extra energy to make it through the day, and I give it back to him in the same way.

It was hard to put the papers down. It was like a spark of their energy, still alive in the words they wrote to each other and about each other. But, tomorrow I would have to let go and send them off to the society. I will make a copies of the originals to keep, and store them carefully in their box for the next generation who wanted a glimpse into the past lives of their ancestors. They, too, could connect and feel the energy of past lives flow through the papers of all who wrote, read, and touched the documents that would lay in front of them one day. The night was creeping ever closer to the middle and I hadn't gone to sleep, so I put the papers aside and went to bed for a few hours.

Chapter Nine

The next morning arrived before I was ready to get up, but I managed to make my way out of bed and into the kitchen to start a much needed pot of coffee. I hadn't been up five minutes and hadn't gotten that first cup before Keith was calling. He would be coming home in three days if everything went as planned. I was so excited! We would be back in each other's arms again soon, and we would be able to look deep within the other's soul, creating and exploding within from all the energy that would be flowing between us and around us. I was refreshed at the thought of his return to me and our home that we have now shared for over seventeen years together. It still felt as though I met him only yesterday, and yet, like I had known him longer than my life on earth at the same time.

I remember a few years before I met Keith, my father told me out of the blue that I would never find what I was seeking. I hadn't thought I was seeking anything. It wasn't until I met Keith that I knew what he was talking about, and fortunately how wrong he was. I had wanted to tell my father how wrong he was but I never did see him again before he died. I thought how sad his life was and how he was one of the people whose soul was like a robber. He had left this world without finding what he was seeking in his life. I had not been seeking anything and found what I didn't know was missing. I guess somehow my father knew my soul was seeking its other half to make me whole as he was searching, and I think everybody is in their lives. Some souls are so entwined in their paths in life that someday their souls will meld into one and the energy will become part of the universe to help guide and direct others on their journeys through life.

Now, with a few cups of coffee in me and the day passing by deep in thought, I got all the documents prepared to mail off to the Mayflower Society. I headed out to put the package in the mailbox just before the postman was due. Then, it was back into the house to clean the breakfast dishes and take a short walk on the beach. I needed to head into town to do some much needed grocery shopping before Keith got home. It was a lovely warm day for December, but I knew the winter winds could change course and turn cold in a moment. So I grabbed a jacket, a scarf, and hat to go out to take a short walk before I missed the beauty in the sky and the warmth of the sun shining.

I walked past the rock I had spent so many days on in the past weeks but felt no draw towards it, I just wanted to walk. I thought with my copies sent off and original documents packed neatly back in their box, shut up in the top of the closet, that the connection to the tides and winds that had drawn me to sit upon the rock at the ocean's edge and take me back to the past was gone. I walked on for a while and then turned to head home when the winds picked up. I stopped to put my coat on when I heard a voice calling me.

I tried to ignore it but with every step closer I got to the rock the louder the voice became; to the point I could not ignore it any longer. It would be like Keith calling out to me and not answering him, I couldn't do it. So I stopped, and sat upon the rock, and listened as the voice called again, "My love, where are you my love?"

I wondered who could be calling now, and then I was drawn back to Clara. They had married and had their children. They were grown and off living their lives. Clara's parents were gone and it was just her and William now. Their children lived in the same town and had children of their own. They would come over once a week and have dinner with them. But for the most part it was just William and Clara. They seemed happy together. As happy as they were from the first moment they met, from what I had read. They would still go to the lake where they first professed their love for each other on warm days a few times a year. They didn't row out in the boat anymore, William's strength was failing him and he hurt for days the last time he tried it. They had lunch at a picnic table now, instead of spreading out a blanket on the ground. Their bodies were old. But the energy deep in their souls was as strong as ever, and their inner selves still felt young with a zest for life as if they were still twenty years-old. They would sometimes sit and talk about their long life together, and sometimes they would sit quietly looking into each other's eyes with the love-light still shining brightly as their two souls conversed with each other without words.

But now their souls spoke differently to each other. They cherished every minute they had left together on this earth, as if making plans for the next time their souls would meet and how to find each other in the next life without knowing where to look. All of a sudden, I was back in the moment but

I didn't hurry home, I sat there sad at the thought

their souls were saying goodbye to each other, even

if only for a brief time, but knowing at the same

time they were making plans for the time their souls

would meet again. Neither Clara nor William were

aware, presently what their souls were talking

about, but they still felt the closeness of the moment

they shared and the life they had together and the

love they still had now. I wondered why I was

supposed to see that. Was it to see Clara and

William at the completion of their life cycle

together? Or, was it to understand how two souls

could make further plans to be together without the

two people consciously knowing. I was sad to see

them in the last stage of life, but happy at the same

time with the insight that the part that made them

who they were would not die when their bodies

failed them. But, would transform and come back into the world again with a new breath of life, spirits calling out to find one another yet again. They would be wiser spirits for what they encountered with each and every life they lived on earth. I got up off the rock with that thought and made my way toward home. It was still early enough in the day to get to the grocery store and home before the darkness and coldness of a December night took over.

Now back home from the long day at the shores edge and the trip to the store. I sat at the counter eating my dinner I just prepared, waiting for Keith to call as I reflected on the day and the past few weeks since Keith had been gone. The glimpses into the past lives of my relatives, or the lives we might have lead, I wasn't really sure which. Either way it had been surreal to sit at the ocean's edge and get those glimpses into the past. That night I awoke to what I thought was thunder, I got out of the bed and went to the window. The sky was clear and the moonlight is shining upon the ocean. The waves crashed hard and strong upon the edge of the shore. As if the waves we're bringing forth a terrible storm, but the sky was clear and the moon bright in the sky. The storm must have been far out to sea. I made my way in the dim light of the hall to the living room and started shuffling through a box of family documents, I found a journal hidden at the bottom. I sat down upon the couch with the journal in hand, I was admiring the beautiful old rugged leather cover. I then put the journal up to my nose and took a deep breath, I wanted to see if the leather still held its scent. Then holding the journal in my hands wanting to open it and start reading, but I was tired and my eyes were heavy. I laid my head onto the pillow beside me and fell asleep until morning caught me off guard as the sun's warmth fell upon my face. I found it hard to sleep soundly since Keith had been away, restlessness seemed to set in the longer he was gone.

This morning I planned to head to the beach early. The weather forecast called for a beautiful morning with a shower late in the day. I wanted to make the most of the early part of the day outside. I drank a cup of coffee and grabbed a quick bite of toast. I could see out the window the ocean waves were calm as seagulls busily looked for food on the shoreline. I was eager to see what the day held for me. I packed a bag and head out to make the short walk to the shore. I found a great place to put my chair and planted an umbrella in the sand. I sat and gazed out into the calmness of the waves and thought the wind and the sea wouldn't likely take me to days gone by as they have done so often lately.

I brought the journal with me to read. The journal about Matthew's life was written in the middle to late 1800s. There were many stories about the struggles and heartaches he endured as well as his greatest joys, and the one true love he found.

Just as the wind and waves brought the past to life, the journal that was before me also gave me the connections to the life of Matthew, how he lived and made his way through life. As I read the accounts of his life, I saw he was a man that enjoyed life and had great principles. A man that tried to make the most out of every moment. He didn't want to waste a minute of living. Matthew's parents died when he was 17 years-old right in front of him. A man robbed his parents and shot them. Matthew grabbed the gun out of the man's hand and killed him.

They lived in Texas in what was called the Irish flats. The outlaw had been robbing and killing hard-working families in the area for several months. He thought the Irish community was easy-picking since most of the folks there were strangers in this growing new world. But that night he was mistaken. He would no longer pray on or hurt anyone in this community, or any other for that matter.

Matthew's brother, John, heard the shot from next door, at his place, and came running into the house. John, devastated by what he found, checked to see if his parents were still alive, but found that neither one had survived the shooting. Everyone gathered to find out what was going on at this point. John went over to his brother Matthew sitting on the floor with his head down.

"What happened?" He cried out.

It took a few moments for John to get through to his brother. Matthew was distraught, not only for losing both of his parents, in a split second, but also for killing a person. Even though it was the man that took the life of his parents, it would take time before he could sort through all the emotions he felt. The sheriff came and considered the outlaw's killing justifiable.

In the days that followed, John decided to go back to his homeland with his wife and young daughter. His wife's parents were still in Ireland and she was home sick. John felt it would be safer for his family back there. Maggie, his wife, hoped her mother and father, and their daughter Lilly, would get to live near her grandparents. John tried to convince his brother to go back with them, but Matthew was determined to make it in America. He told John his parents wanted nothing more than to make America their new home, and give them the opportunities they lacked in the Ireland.

The brothers decided their paths in life would be going in different directions. John was heading back to their homeland and Matthew was going to stay in America. Matthew went to the port with John, Maggie, and Lilly to send them off and wish them well. They all hugged as they said goodbye and promised to write each other. The brothers looked at each other as if they knew their paths would never cross again in person, only through letters from time to time. They said their final goodbyes and Matthew watched as the ship set sail to make the journey across the Atlantic.

Matthew went home and made preparations to head out on the Chisholm Trail. He collected a few things he treasured most and packed what he thought he needed to survive on the open range. He signed up to be part of a cattle drive from Texas to Wyoming. Even though his emotions were still raw, he still felt a little excitement about his new direction in life, and the adventures he imagined were ahead of him. His life's path was really just starting to be formed. All alone in this new world, and without any family, he was determined more than ever, to make it and prove to himself that his parent's dreams we're not in vain. Matthew resolved to show everyone that he could make of himself whatever he wanted. He knew he would miss his brother, the only family he had left, and wished that he would have stayed and made a go of it, but he understood why his brother decided to return to Ireland.

Matthew knew he wouldn't be able to take much with him on the trail, so he only kept a few small things that belonged to his mother and father. They didn't have any value but the items meant a lot to them, and now meant even more to him. The rest of his parent's belongings he let his brother and sister-in-law have. They would take most of what they brought to America back home where it came from.

A locket with his mother's picture in it, his father's pocket watch, and his father's journal was all he kept. Matthew had been reading his father's journal since he passed. It comforted him to read his father's thoughts and the life experiences he shared. It explained a lot about how his father lived. His father had been writing in this journal as long as he could remember. Matthew's mother told him once his father started the day they got married and had written in it every day since. Some days it was a brief thought or expression and other days he sat and wrote for hours. She said he always told her she could read it anytime she wanted.

She told him, "When we are old and gray I will read your journal but not till then."

My mother never got to read about his thoughts or dreams. She never read the words expressing how he felt or the way he loved and adored her. She knew in many other ways, by the way he looked at her, or a gentle touch. We all could see the love our parents had for each other. Still, he wished his mother could have had the chance to reach the age where she would have read the words that expressed just how deeply she was cherished.

As Matthew read his father's journal, he was able to get a sense his father's deepest thoughts and how he perceived life. He read it so many times he memorized each and every word. All he had left of his father's was a timepiece, the memories, and this written account of how he lived up to the moment of his death. It angered him to know he had been robbed of the many entries that would forever be left empty in his journal. He thought of his father and mother growing old together, watching their children mature, and make their own way in life. He thought of the grandchildren they would never get to meet and his father would never get to write about. His father had been excited about John getting married, starting a family, and the birth of his first granddaughter. For a moment Matthew pauses and realized his father and mother would never meet the woman he would eventually marry or the children he and his wife would one day have. It saddened him to know he would never get to experience or read about his father's love for his family and children.

Matthew decided he would keep a written account of his life so he could pass on to his family, his stories, thoughts and dreams. He had learned the importance of a journal and why his father kept one. Matthew realized the impact a journal could have on the generations to come.

Reading his father's journal, he learned of the character, values and love of life his parents shared. The joys and sorrows they faced and how they got through them. He read the messages they left to their children. Matthew was determined not be bitter, instead he would focus on the constructive aspects of his parents, hoping to have a positive impact on people. He vowed to live the best and most honorable life he could. Matthew wanted to leave footprints of his life that his family would be proud of. The ideal example demonstrated by his father and mother left a lasting impression on him. He felt obligated to live his life to the same high standards his parents had.

Matthew stopped at the general store before meeting up with the group of cowboys he would work with on the cattle drive. He wanted to pick up his own journal and some pencils to write with, along with a few other supplies. Then he walked over to meet the foreman and a few members of the crew that had already gathered. When the whole group assembled they made their way to the stockyard and looked over the cattle they were hired to take north. The foreman knew the story about the tragedy Matthew had just went through and how young he was. He admired Matthew for his determination to forge forward and took him under his wing. He knew if Matthew chose to stay on and learn from him, someday he could be a great cattle driver. He would have to stay the course and not be lead a stray by the seedy characters that often signed on to cattle drives. He wanted to see Matthew make it.

Matthew started writing in his journal the first night and continued from then on. He talked about how hard the first day was and how he liked the foreman and made friends with him. Matthew was eager to learn and understand everything there was about cattle driving. As the years passed he became a cattle driver in his own right. He purchased some land in Nebraska and made plans to build a house and own his own cattle ranch. He worked on the trail as much as he could and in the off season he worked on his land and started building a house. All the money he made went into the ranch and cattle. Eventually, Matthew hired a ranch foreman to tend to his cattle and watch over the ranch until he returned. He planned on two more years of running cattle for others then he would settle down to the ranch and tend his own cattle. By then his herd would be large enough he would only have time to take his own cattle up the trail.

The two years went by and everything went as planned. Over time, Matthew had selectively picked the finest cattle and built one of the best herds ever accumulated. He built a remarkable ranch and became one of the most significant cattle owners in Nebraska. One day, Matthew went into town to buy some supplies and met Emma at the general store. She was with her father, which Matthew had met many times before, but he didn't know he had a daughter, and especially such a beautiful one. Her father was a lawyer and handled many of Matthew's business affairs, but somehow the two had never met, until now. They hit it off and before spring turned to fall they were planning to get married. I could tell by his writing how much he adored and loved Emma. He wrote in his journal that he fell in love with Emma the moment he laid eyes on her. Meeting her caused Matthew to have flashbacks of the memories his father wrote about his mother. His father's journal expressed many times how she was the one and only love for him. He hadn't thought much of his father's journal for a few years now. He was busy working towards his goals and dreams. Time had helped heal most of his wounds that haunted him. For the first couple of years after it happened, Matthew would often wake-up from nightmares, reliving the terrible day.

He hadn't written or heard from his brother in over a year and thought now would be a great time to write. Matthew invited John and Maggie to the wedding and asked them to bring their daughters. They were up to three the last Matthew heard. He also offered John a home on the ranch if he wanted to try a new start here again. His brother quickly wrote back that he was happy for him and wished Matthew and his soon-to-be new bride a wonderful life together, but they wouldn't be able to make the trip. John told Matthew the wounds of what happened never healed for him, that maybe if he had stayed, things would have turned out differently and he could've moved beyond it. But, leaving so soon after the death of their parents left John with only sad memories of this country and he doubted he would ever return. Matthew tried to assure him that it was different where he was but to no avail. Matthew knew at that moment he would never see his brother again. He thought when his brother left there was still a chance that one day he and family might come back and try again, but now he knew his dream of being reunited with John was over.

He turned his attention to Emma and their upcoming plan to marry. Emma was his life now. He knew they would have a good life together, and looked forward to the day he could have a family of his own. For a long time, Matthew dreamed of the day he would have a wife and children—someone to carry on his name. His thoughts often led him to the dream of having a family to share life with, someone to pass a legacy on to.

Their wedding day couldn't get here fast enough. He wrote in his journal how he loved Emma's beautiful blue eyes and her long auburn hair and how soft-spoken her voice was. She was tall with a beautiful figure. He couldn't wait to hold her in his arms and kiss her sweet lips. He wrote about how nervous he was in anticipation of their wedding night. He couldn't recall the last time he we so anxious. Matthew always felt confident, being nervous was a feeling he seldom experienced. He wanted everything to be perfect. All his days of running cattle had roughened his hands and he didn't want the calluses to scratch her smooth skin. Matthew went to the tool shed, got a file he used to sharpen his axes and filed the rough calluses off his hands. Then, he took some lye soap and scrubbed and soaked them in buttermilk. He never wanted to hurt Emma in any way, even in touching her tender soft skin.

It worked, and his fears of scratching her were over, but he was still nervous about their first night together. Would Emma approve of how he touched her? When would be the appropriate time to make love to her? There were so many things Matthew wanted to do right, but he had no experience. He finally decided to try to not worry about it. He knew worry would certainly work against him. He was going to take the approach of going slow and gentle, and hoped Emma approved.

The day finally arrived. Today, he would make Emma his wife. The whole town came out for their wedding. But Matthew only focused on Emma. After the ceremony there was a party for them, which they stayed longer for than either of them wanted to. It was a long day of excitement and as soon as the newlyweds felt it appropriate, they left, albeit earlier than most. Matthew took Emma by the arm and they said their goodbyes to all her family and their friends and headed to the ranch. They glowed outwardly with the love-light in their eyes. The trip to the ranch seemed longer to Matthew than ever before. He couldn't wait to be alone, to hold Emma in his arms, like he had dreamed of for months.

Matthew re-read parts of his father's journal the night before. He was searching for the parts where his father expressed how much he loved his mother and how gently he treated her. When

Matthew was younger these parts of the journal embarrassed him, but now he was grateful that his father had written and expressed his emotions and the love he had for his mother. It told him how much they truly loved each other and that they were able to express, not only with words, but in their actions, even if in the smallest of ways. The pages now gave Matthew a sense of how to express to Emma how much he loved her. He wanted to give Emma every part of him wholly and unconditionally. His father had given him a sort of how-to-guide, at least to get started. How to treat his new bride with love and respect, gentleness and kindness. Not that Matthew didn't already know most of that on his own. It was the small things his father mentioned in his journal on how he would always greet his wife with a warm gentle kiss every morning and every night before they laid their heads down to sleep. That he would not take for granted how he loved to look into her beautiful blue eyes and loved her smile. Even the way she showed a total sense of assurance and love in the way she interacted with the children as she gently talked to them and taught those lessons. Matthew wanted to show the same love to Emma.

When they finally made it to the ranch Matthew could hardly contain his need to take Emma into the house and lay her on the bed, undress her, and make love to her until the morning sun rose into the sky. But he knew he would have to give her a few moments after the ride in the carriage to freshen up. He knew he needed a few moments himself. So after helping her down from the carriage and taking her into the house, he ran and got some fresh water, enough to fill two basins. He came back in to see her walking around the house, looking at everything intently. Matthew let her know that it was her home now and she could move all the things in the house out and put her things in to set up the house any way she wanted. He told Emma he would take the fresh water up to the bedroom and put it into the basin so she could freshen up. He would clean up in the kitchen. He led her up the stairs and showed her around. He showed her their bedroom, and expressed again that she could rearrange the whole house any way she felt fit. He closed the door behind him to give her some privacy. He knew in just a little while they would both be laying together with nothing on, completely vulnerable to being touched, kissed, and looked at by the other's eyes like never before. His anxiety had been replaced by a strong desire to hold her in his arms and completely immerse their two bodies into one like their souls have already done. Matthew knew from then on that they would be complete in body and spirit for the first time.

Twenty minutes passed since he had left Emma in the bedroom to freshen up. Matthew decided to make his way back up the stairs to the bedroom. As he knocked on the door, he heard Emma respond with her sweet voice, "Come in Matthew and join me in the bed."

Matthew didn't hesitate to her request. As he walked across the room, he was undressing. He stood before his new bride naked and climbed into bed. It wouldn't be until much later, that Matthew would realize his plan to take it slow and gentle was derailed by Emma's invitation to join her in bed. Just to hear her speak the words triggered an animal like reaction.

Emma was dressed in a new nightgown she had a lady in town make for her wedding night. He told her as he undressed her how beautiful she looked lying on their bed. He kissed her gently but passionately as he continued to undress her. Emma wrapped her arms around his shoulders and started to feel his body as her fingers explored the form of her husband. Both were touching and feeling each other's bodies as they kissed passionately. Matthew caressed Emma's breast, stopped kissing her lips and worked his way down her neck. He moved his body on top of hers as he put her fully erect nipple in his mouth, and continued caressing her other breast. He put himself inside her and repeatedly, but gently thrust himself into her body. It didn't take long before their bodies exploded with passion. Matthew rolling over onto his back, rolling Emma with him, laying her head upon his chest. They laid there for hours, separating just enough to look into each other's eyes talking, kissing, and making love over and over, keeping their bodies locked around each other.

As I read Matthew's journal, it reminded me of first night Keith and I made love. I felt completely connected to Emma and Matthew. Feeling all the emotions and love they had for each other. It was as if Keith and I were Matthew and Emma. I wondered if this was a life we lived before. As I read the words Matthew wrote on the pages of the journal, I couldn't help but feel a strong correlation with their lives and my own.

The morning came too quickly for Matthew and Emma. They reluctantly made their way out of bed to start their first full day as husband and wife. They cleaned up and Matthew left Emma in the bedroom to give her time to finish dressing and brush her long hair. He ran out to get firewood and started a fire in the fireplace and the stove. Emma came down and started making breakfast. Matthew showed her where everything was in the kitchen. Again, he told her she could rearrange everything wherever she wanted. Emma listened as he talked while she prepared their breakfast. He told her about building the house in stages when he wasn't on a cattle drive and how many times he changed the plans. He told her he would even rearrange or add rooms to the house if she wanted him to.

They we're both quite hungry and couldn't wait to eat. The full pot of coffee was nearly gone by the time the food finished up in the frying pan. When breakfast was ready they sat down at the kitchen table to eat. They talked and stared into each other's eyes as they planned their day and life together.

After breakfast, Matthew gathered some of his ranch hands to go into town to get Emma's belongings from her parent's house. It was all packed and ready before Matthew arrived. Emma's father and mother were expecting him and met him at the door. They helped load her things into the wagon. Matthew told them Emma sent her love and would come to town in a few days to see them. They smiled and sent their love back.

Matthew didn't stay much longer than it took to get the wagon loaded. He didn't want to leave Emma too long, but he also knew she needed a little time to herself. With everything on the wagon, they headed back towards the ranch. Matthew rode on ahead, leaving the ranch hands to bring the buckboard at a slower pace. He planned to cut across country on the return trip which allowed him to get back as soon as he could. Every moment away that morning was like a lifetime to him. As he went around the bend, turning into the ranch entrance, he could see Emma sitting on the porch swing awaiting his return. He rode straight up to the porch, jumped off his horse and pulled Emma off of the porch swing into his arms. He kissed her with the same passion as he had the night before. They sat down in the swing together and waited for the buckboard to arrive. He already instructed his hired help that they would be helping him and Emma set up her things in the house. They were to help place everything where she wanted it and help move out anything Emma didn't want in the house. The men road into the ranch about a half an hour later. They pulled the buckboard up to the front porch to start unloading Emma's things. Emma's eyes filled with excitement as her things were being unloaded and put on the porch.

"What would you like moved out of the house?" Matthew asked.

"Well, would you mind if we used the dresser and chest of drawers for our bedroom, and moved the ones currently in there to the spare bedroom?" she asked, smoothing the front of her cotton dress.

"Not at all, my love," he said and kissed her cheek before turning to his ranch-hands. "You heard the lady of the house, boys. Let's get moving."

She thanked them as they passed her on the porch carrying the heavy furniture. By the time they got back downstairs she had her mind made up where she wanted everything and what she wanted removed. It didn't take the three men long before they had everything where she wanted it. She chased the men out of the house to start putting the kitchen together, adding her things, and rearranging everything so it was easily found when needed.

Matthew went back to the porch swing as happy as he could be. He enjoyed listening to the clanging of pots and pans, and the clinking of glasses as his wife worked away in their home. He waited on the porch just in case she needed him for anything. He didn't want to be too far away.

He was thinking about their wedding night and their two bodies connecting and merging into one, when Emma came to the door to call him to lunch. He jumped to his feet and took her by the hand as they walked to the table. After lunch they went for a walk down near the river, just below the stables. She wanted to see the barn, the toolshed, and all the other surrounding buildings around the house.

They talked, walked, and swung on the porch swing as early evening came, Emma went in to start dinner while Mathew gathered firewood for the stove. He brought extra wood into the house just in case he would need to stoke the fireplace in the middle of the night. It was early fall and the weather in Nebraska changed quickly with a strong wind from the Dakotas. For dinner they had leftovers from lunch. Matthew stayed and talked in the kitchen while Emma straighten up.

After dinner they went into the sitting room for a little while until Matthew asked Emma if she was ready for bed. She quickly agreed, and taking her by the hand, led her to the bottom of the stairs. He told her he had already put clean water in the basin for her and he would give her time to clean up while he washed up downstairs again. Emma rushed upstairs to the bedroom. She undressed and cleaned her body from head to toe. She let her hair down and brushed it over her shoulders, and then put her gown on, climbing into bed and waited for Matthew. Tonight he went straight in without knocking. His bride was now his wife and now one in spirit and body. He had seen every part of her body, and she his. Matthew no longer felt any awkwardness about being naked in front of Emma.

He crossed the room, undressing himself again, so by the time he reached the bed he was naked, and climb right into bed. Matthew kissed Emma on the lips and wrapped his arms around her as she touched his chest. Emma moved her hands downward, caressing and exploring every inch of Matthew's body. He again found himself exploring her body as he continued to kiss her. His mouth alternated between her lips and breast. Then he climbed on top of her and with more urgency than the night before, started making love to her. She grabbed onto his waist and pulled him closer with each thrust into her body until they exploded from the passion. Matthew rolled onto his back with care as he pulled Emma closer. Stroking her hair, removing it from her eyes, he kissed her forehead. As he gently kissed her lips telling her he loved her. She rubbed her hand over his chest, kissed his chest, and laid her head on him as if she was trying to get as close as possible. He loved the way she made love with him. They fell asleep, holding each other closely.

Morning came quickly but neither of them hurry to get up. Both loved being in each other's arms and were in no hurry to separate and get the day started. They cuddled together, talking, and kissing. Before they knew it they we're making love. When they made their way out of each other's arms, and out of bed. They dressed and went downstairs.

As Emma started breakfast, they drank coffee and talked of the day's plans. They decided to ride into town to pick up some things from the general store: flour, sugar, baking supplies, coffee, and so on. They planned to stop by and see Emma's mother and father for a brief visit before heading home.

They made it to her parent's house and her mother insisted they have lunch and a piece of pie. She had just taken Emma's favorite cream pie out of the oven. Her mother looked her daughter in the eyes, and at the glow about her, knowing Emma had found her soulmate, as she had so many years ago. She knew her daughter would be well taken care of by Matthew and that he would lay his own life down for her. There was nothing more a mother could ask for than to see her child happy and in love.

The years went by swiftly for Emma and Matthew. As Matthew and Emma were now welcoming the birth of their third child. Life was good and their love grew stronger with each passing year, as they watched their children Harper, Julia and Preston

Matthew was faithful, like his father, to write in his journal. He felt it would be helpful one day for his children and generations to come. He wanted them to get a glimpse into his life and some into his father's life, too. He wanted to share his understanding of love and the joy of finding his soulmate.

Matthew and Emma raised their children on the ranch. They loved watching their children grow into young adults. It wasn't long before they were getting married and having children of their own. Matthew wrote about the joys of becoming a father. He especially enjoyed being there for his children as they grew into adulthood and went out to carve their own paths in life with their families. They all stayed close and visited often. Matthew and Emma were fortunate to see their grandchildren as they grew, something Matthew always felt his parents had been robbed of.

Emma and Matthew grew old together, keeping the love-light in their hearts and souls for each other. Then the day came, Matthew awoke in the middle of the night, looked over at Emma, and realized she was not breathing. He was devastated his Emma was gone. He laid in bed holding her in his arms, crying, begging her to come back, at the same time saying goodbye to her.

That was the last entry in Matthew's journal. I didn't know if he felt without Emma there was nothing to write about or if he died shortly after from a broken heart. As I sat in my chair at the beach, pondering what happened to Matthew after Emma's death, I looked up to see the waves rushing the shore and turning more powerful than I ever saw them before. I felt as if Matthew caused such powerful waves to let me know he was there, and the love of Emma was a love that never died even when their bodies gave out their spirit continued on.

Again, I felt as if the spirit of Emma and Matthew lived within Keith and me.

The waves were forceful against the shore and I was losing daylight. I gathered my things and headed back to the house. As I approached the back door, I heard the phone ringing. I answered it as quickly as I could. It was Keith.

"I was concerned about you. I had a strange feeling about the waves and the ocean today and knew you were going to be at the beach and got worried. I tried calling several times," he said in a rush.

"Oh, I found another journal and since it was an unusually warm day for this time of the year, I took it with me to the beach to read. The journal was about the love of Matthew and Emma. I felt strangely connected to them, as if it was us in a former life. When I finished reading the waves became more forcefully than I had ever seen before. But, don't worry. I was in no danger and came straight to the house when I realized how powerful the waves and wind had grown," I said more breathless than I realized I was.

"Are you sure you're okay?" I could feel the concern in his voice.

"Yes. Please, don't worry. I'm safe at home now and it has been a long day. I'm going to eat something and take a long hot bath. Then, I plan to relax by the fire. Maybe I'll go to bed early, or, grab a canvas and paint. I feel so wound up. I needed to find a way to unwind and shake off all the powerful emotions of the day," I waved my hands as I spoke even though he couldn't see me through the phone.

"That sounds like a great idea. I'll let you rest now that I know you're safe. I'm going to work on some sketches and make some final changes tonight. I'll call first thing in the morning," he sighed. "I wish I was already home with you. I hate leaving you alone for so long. And, I miss your touch and being in each other's arms."

"I miss all that, too babe. I love you."

I soaked in the tub for an hour, grabbed a snack and went to sit by the fire. I began a rough sketch, outlining a scene I wanted to paint. Before I even got the background down I decided I was too tired and ready for bed. Wore out from the day, I made it into the bed and thought I would fall fast asleep, but sleep escaped me as my thoughts longed to have my husband by my side with his arm drawing me in close to his body. I finally found myself falling into a deep sleep around two a.m., and waking up late. I busied myself for Keith's return. Today was the day he would return home to me, and my heart and soul were leaping in anticipation. It felt unsettled as it had the day we met. In just a few hours we would be back in each other's arms, holding each other close, and looking into each other's eyes, reconnecting our souls together and then our bodies. We would make love to each other for days as we had at the beginning of our life together. We would talk of the time apart and look at pictures of the sculpture he had done. We would talk of my days walking and sitting on the beach while he was gone. We would reconnect in every way, as if never parting. I would tell him that I finished the research for the Mayflower Society and was waiting for them to send me my membership papers. My mom was growing closer to the end of her time on earth and I wanted her to be able to see for herself that the task near and dear to her heart was finally complete. I think that stories about her life should be put into the box of papers and documents of the family to someday be found by future generations, to give them a glimpse into the life she led and the footprints she left.

I decided that the days I spent on the beach while Keith was gone were awaken by my research. When you look back into the past and read about those that came before, they forever leave a mark, in a quest for love of family and history.

The lives they lived, the footprints they left on this earth, the struggles they went through from our first generation in America to me. Our history showed the footprints my family made, including the wars they fought for our freedom, from the first wars fought on these lands to the later ones overseas. They put their lives on the line, in hopes that the generations after them would have a more perfect life than they'd had. How can we not take the time out of what we call our busy lives to look back on a personal level, to the generations of our family that came before us? Sometimes I think the box and papers of the past should be thought about on a more frequent basis to keep us grounded, and remind us what real life is truly about. Not the instant gratification we all seem to think we deserve. Not to live in the past or the future, but to live in the moment, without the sense of entitlement. I have a greater respect for those who came before me. The journey for the truth to the *Mayflower* story encompassed my life for a moment. The journey was great and of great satisfaction for my mother. To have a dream of her mother's fulfilled was a sweet reward for me. I was fulfilling two generation's dreams. I had learned so much more than I ever thought possible about so many generations. It would take me a lifetime just to take pen in hand and write all the stories of their lives.

My Keith will be home today.

I finished up last minute things around the house before I left for the airport to get him. I grabbed my coat and hat and stop for a moment in front of the window, looking out to the ocean and wondered if the voices of the past would be quiet and still now. I was saddened at the thought of never hearing them again. I hoped they would come again and share with me more of the lives they have led through centuries and generations.

I was brought back to the moment and I hurry out the door. I wanted to arrive at the airport before Keith's plane touches down. It didn't take long before I arrived and watched the plane land and taxi to the gate. I felt my soul jump with excitement, knowing it would reconnect with Keith's in just a few moments. Then, I saw him as he exited the plane and came down the ramp and into the airport terminal. I immediately started to make my way to him, waiting for the moment our eyes and souls were able to reconnect to each other.

And in that very moment our eyes connect, I immediately felt the warmth of his soul reaching out to me, comforting me like a warm blanket on a cold December day. Then the moment came when our bodies reach out to each other and he took me into his arms. All the aching and longing for each other's touch disappeared, fading away in the comfort of the now.

We gathered Keith's bags and made our way to the car, and then home. When we reached the house and got out of the car, Keith stood and paused.

He said, "I missed our home and want to take it all in for a moment. It's like a friend welcoming me home from a long journey. Standing steadfast in the same place, like an anchor thrown into the ocean to hold a ship from drifting off."

Then he made his way to the door where I stood, waiting for him so we could enter our home together. He took me by the hand. With his free hand he opened the door and took a deep breath as he walked into the house. He wanted to smell the scents we had created in the house over the many years that made our house our home. He then took me into his arms and we made our way to our bedroom. He undressed me, then himself, and he looked deep within my eyes, reaching for my soul, wanting to reconnect our bodies back together like our souls had been reconnected.

Keith climbed upon me and thrust himself within me as we entwined our bodies together, not knowing where one started and the other ended, until our bodies exploded with shared pleasure. Keith then drew me into his arms laying my head upon his chest, slowly brushing my long hair between his figures, as we lay together for hours, tenderly caressing each other's bodies without a word being spoken, living in the moment, together with a sense of our love for each other encompassing the whole room.

Evening fell so we got up to make dinner and talk. I had already prepared a few of Keith's favorite foods earlier in the day. We eat and we talk. We smiled and look deep within each other's eyes. It is as if we refilled every sense that had been lacking since we had been away from each other. After eating we went to the living room and Keith lit a fire like he did first time I entered our home.

He said he had reflected on our lives together while he was away and that the reflection didn't come close to the reality of it. Then he took me into his arms and laid me down on the couch and made love to me over and over again as he did those many years ago. But every time Keith made love to me felt like the first time. We spent the whole night in each other's arms. We had fallen asleep. Next thing I knew he hugged me and said, "Good morning, my love."

We finished the embrace and gathered our clothes to go to the bathroom for a shower and to put on fresh clothes. We made our way to the kitchen for coffee and breakfast. I couldn't think of a better way to start the morning than with Keith home again and right across from me having coffee, talking and listening to each other. We sat and talked for hours, him telling me his tales of Canada, and me speaking of my days at the edge of the ocean. We laughed as we shared our stories.

We decided to start planning our next trip to Europe for the spring. It had been a few years since our last trip. We had felt a longing to make a return. It was warm and inviting to us. There was also a sense of going home when we went to Europe, as if a long ago past greeted us as we arrived. We usually flew to Paris and spent a few days there before heading south to a small town near Provence. We travelled mostly on the rail system that gently glided across the tracks as we looked at the landscape. The train passed many quaint towns along the way as we headed to our destinations, some small towns high in the mountains, some on the shores of the Mediterranean Sea. Then, we would head off to Italy and on to Switzerland. I loved to stand on top of the mountains in Switzerland and look at the endless snow covered mountains that slowly fade into the clouds that form around them. There was so much to take in visually that it seemed hard for the brain to compute it all at once. They looked like the rocks on the edge of the sea that are gray in color with a white covering that looked as if someone climbed the hills above and spilled buckets of paint onto them. The thought of going back makes me wonder, if I stood on the shore of the Mediterranean would I hear the voices of other ancestors? Or, would the voices from many centuries be quieted by time, unable to send messages in the winds and the waves? Perhaps all the voices could do now is to leave the traces of themselves in the warm, welcoming feeling through the mists of the sea gently flowing onto our faces as if to give a kiss of welcome home.

Keith and I have been fortunate enough to travel and adventure throughout Europe and America over the years together. We were careful to not take any of it for granted or with a sense of entitlement. Only when we arrived to stand at the edge of the sea would I know if the voices of my ancestors were able to still call out, even if so faintly but enough to be heard if I stood quiet enough. I looked forward to our trip. Would it be the sense of welcoming, or would I get to hear the voices in the winds and waves telling me of their lives past?

We sat at the table most of the morning making plans for the trip. Now, we were going to take a walk at our ocean's edge. Keith missed our walks together along the shore, as had I. But the walks would hold a little more meaning to them since the times I stood and sat alone while he was gone.

As we made our way to the shore Keith asked, "Do you think I will hear the voices of my ancestors calling out to me as they have for you?"

I answered, "I don't know. I have no answer to why I was able to. Just a few theories."

Today was windy and cold and we didn't stay on the shore long before we headed back home to warm by the fire.

Keith said, "I think you were given a glimpse into the past that I won't get. I think, for whatever reason, you were given the opportunity but I won't have the same chance. You should write it down, to give to the grandchildren and to hand down for decades to come. They might also venture to the ocean's edge decades and centuries in the future to listen to what the wind and waves will bring to them as they have to you, my love."

"I hoped you are right. I hope they will be able to get a vision and glimpse into our life together and see how we loved and laughed and lived. I hope they will have the chance to see how happy and in love we were together since the moment we met. I hope they will read everything handed down in the family and that just reading the letters and the messages will connect them closer to their roots and their history," I said squeezing his hand with a mixture of excitement and contentment. "I hope they wonder what kind of ancestors came before them? What footprints have they left behind for others to follow, like a road map for how to be happy and have a sense of purpose in life, to give it meaning not only to self but to others?"

We sat by the fire and talked and watched as the fire's glow turned to faint embers. We were tired from the day and went to bed early to hold each other close as we fell asleep. We woke early with the bright sunshine creeping through the window. After breakfast we went out to the studio. Keith worked on a sculpture he would have bronzed and I worked on a painting of the lavender fields in France from my memories as I stood upon a hillside. As I paint them it excited me. I couldn't wait for our trip to get here so we could stand on that hillside again and look out onto the meadow of lavender, purples of every shade, from the shadows of light and the reflections of the clouds. How I long for winter's end and the coming of spring.

The days and weeks went by as Keith and I made our way to the studio every day to fill our need to express ourselves through art. Time passed quickly and spring came into bloom in the air and the flowers made their way from the earth to show off their beauty outwardly for everyone to see. The animals brought forth new offspring and everything came to life, awakened from a long slumber. Now that winter had passed us and it was spring, we were ready for our trip to Europe. We finished up our current projects. It had taken a few weeks to get everything done and ready to go. A few more days and we would be on another adventure, making memories together. We were excited and didn't sleep much thinking of all we would see and the people we would meet along the way.

On the day of departure, we woke long before morning's light had a chance to fill the bedroom. We had an early flight. We we're brushing our teeth and hair and making sure we had everything we planned to bring. We got into the kitchen and grabbed a little to eat and a couple cups of coffee, then were off to the airport. We made it there with little time to spare before we boarded the plane.

We had a direct flight so we settled in for a long ride. Keith, always kind, let me put my legs over the top of him and lay my head on his shoulder. I slept most of the way. Keith slept a little but watched movies for the most part. We got a taxi to the hotel. I loved to stay on the left bank, it is close to everything I like to see while there. It became like a second home. Favorite restaurants we liked to eat at, shops we enjoy, and our favorite hotel. The museums were close, along with Notre Dame. Every place we went and everything we did was within walking distance for us. We spent a few days there and then onto Arles. I loved the coliseum there, and walking the path that the old famous painters walked, and standing where they stood to paint their paintings. To see what they saw as they painted their famous works of art. Just to walk the streets and gape in awe at the architecture of the centuries before is amazing in itself. It's like walking through a history picture book but being able to touch and walk inside of them, it was like living in another period in time. The only difference seemed to be the fashion of the day.

We said goodbye to Arles and made our way to the Mediterranean Sea. We went to Avignon first, to marvel at the old historical section, then down to Monaco. I had never seen water anywhere else in the world as blue and transparent than the Mediterranean Sea. The water is so clear the naked eye could see the bottom. We walked the shoreline and I listened for a calling from the winds and waves, straining to hear even a faint voice. But I heard nothing, just the gentle breeze brushing my face and a feeling of welcome. The voices were quieted by time, too far gone to be heard any more. It saddens me to think the stories of their lives are gone. Most have not endured, we only have small fragments and our imaginations must fill in the rest.

But imagination doesn't let you see the true person and know their thoughts and dreams and everyday lives. Were the times they lived in good to them? I am thinking. Did they get the most out of their lives? Did their lives end from sickness or old age? Did they find happiness in their lifetime, or pain and suffering? I have to put the thoughts to bed. I have no way of knowing, I have only questions and nowhere to get the answers. Questions without a path to answers are better left to time. I know parts of my family can be traced back before 1066. But the ones I feel I am being welcomed by, in the kiss of the wind, are the more humble, gentle souls of the families that had little but gave much. I feel that if they were still able to carry stories of their lives through the winds and waves, they would.

Keith and I walked for a while on the beach before heading to our next destination. Our train hugged the shoreline from France to Italy. There was beauty to be had everywhere on the train, with its large windows. It only took a few hours to make our journey. We switched from the high speed train to a local one that slowly moved through the Italian mountains, stopping frequently for locals making their way through their daily lives. We stopped in a Monterosso al Mare, where few spoke anything but Italian. We checked into a hotel converted from an old stone home that looked out over the sea, close to the shore. We had planned this stop at the last minute to immerse ourselves into the daily lives of the people of the Monterosso al Mare, to feel a part of a different culture if, only for a few days, to communicate with others in a language other than our own. We found the people delightful as they went an extra mile to understand our attempts at their language. The people of the Monterosso al Mare seemed to enjoy the company of people from a different culture taking the time to sit with them and experience the beauty and quiet of the town they call home. They must have something special to make a stranger stop to spend time with them. They went out of their way to make the experience special for us.

After a few days it is time to move on to Switzerland. We took a boat ride across the beautiful lake, Lucerne to reach the cog rail train that would take us high up onto the mountain. From there we walked the rest of the way to reach the summit. Keith and I stood in awe at the peak as we watched the clouds float by to cover the mountain top. The other mountain tops were far distant as we slowly made our way down to the tram that would sail us through the sky, back to the base of the mountain. We again made our way across the lake to the village and walked the streets, going into all the small shops serving their specialties of their region. We spent one night here. As beautiful as it is, I feel no sense of connection to this place the way I did France. There is no sense of the inner warmth and love or a welcoming deep within me. The next morning, we awoke early and checked out of the hotel, making our way to the train station, we headed back to Paris before going to England. This is a trip I have been waiting a long time to make. I wanted it to be the last stop so that I would be completely in the moment, not full of anticipation for any other stop on our journey. I wanted my senses to be focused only on the places I stood and my family. Long before I joined the Mayflower Society of Descendants I knew where my family came from. I had always wanted to stand on the shores of Plymouth, England. To stand at the ocean's edge where my ancestors departed for New England and landed at New Plymouth. I heard my ancestors speak in the winds and waves in on the ocean's edge in Plymouth, Massachusetts. Now, I want to see if I would hear and feel my ancestors in the place they departed. I wanted to walk the streets and wander the villages in which they lived. To see if I could feel a sense of them as I walked on the paths they traveled many hundreds of years before. I needed to see if I feel the welcoming in the winds as I did in other parts of Europe. I hoped that here the greeting would be stronger, instead of the faintness in the welcome I felt from the other parts of Europe. My thoughts carried me away, but the plane brought me back to the moment as we landed in England. My heart filled with excitement as we started to disembark the plane and make our way through the terminal to the car we rented. Plymouth, England was a four hour drive. I hoped the scenery would be beautiful as we made our way south of London to Plymouth.

The drive was interesting with Keith having to teach himself to drive on the other side of the road. Neither of us had experience with that. The drive was pleasant once we got out of London and into the rural countryside. We talked about family and the things we had recently experienced. The time flew by. As we made our way into the town, there were many stone buildings lining the road.

The landing in Plymouth, England is the hub for tall ships even today, but you tell that it was once a place for a many ships to stop. I couldn't wait to get settled into our room and make our way down to shore line. I already felt a sense of calling to the ocean's edge, as if I was being beckoned to its shore by the voices in the wind and waves. I couldn't wait to walk the paths of those who came before me. We planned to spend a few moments there today, between the plane ride and the drive, the day was slipping away from us. Tomorrow we would spend the day at the ocean's edge, exploring the town and the small shops that lined the streets. Today was a full one and we were tired and hungry. We talked of the plans for tomorrow as we left the hotel and meandered down the streets to the water. We walked to the edge, feeling as if we were greeted by family as the wind gently brushed our faces, as if to welcome us home from a long journey with a kiss upon our cheeks and hugs that wrapped around us. It brought a warm smile to our faces. For not only did my family board the *Mayflower* in 1620, so did Keith's. By the look on his face, I could see he was feeling as if he was also being welcomed by spirits of the past.

We walked along the shore for a short time, then made our way to a nearby restaurant. We thought it would be a great place to look upon the ocean as we ate dinner. The waiter suggested we get up early before dawn, he said if we wanted to watch the fog roll back to sea with the tide. He went onto say it was amazing site to behold. He said legend has it that before the dawning of the day people say they hear gentle soft spoken voices coming from the fog. Before quietly returning back out to sea with the tide.

We took the waiters advice and woke up hours before daybreak. We hurried to dress and out the door we went. Neither of us wanted to waste a moment getting to the shore. It was eerily quiet outside. The fog was thick and heavy, we could hear the footsteps of an old fisherman making his way home from a night of fishing. As we got closer we could see he carried a basket over his shoulder with his catch of the night and a pole in the other. We said hello as we crossed pass. I thought to myself, does he hear the calling late at night when casting his line into the water as we reach the sea's edge. Now standing hand and hand, Keith and I quietly stand looking at the beauty of the misty fog and listen to the waves crashing the shore before retreating with the fog. Neither of us spoke a word to each other, we gently squeezed each other's hand as we listened.

Dawn was starting to break and the fog was now retreating back out to sea with the tide. I felt warm even in the wet misty cold fog. I felt again as if I was being hugged by someone from the past, but again voices escaped me. Even without hearing anyone, I felt strangely warm and welcomed. I fear their voices have been silenced long ago with no one there to hear. They can now only reach out with spirit to welcome family long gone from England

On the drive back to London, the views were amazing and wonderful. We passed fields of heather that stretched for miles through the country side. We passed quaint cottages that seemed to appear out of nowhere. The cottages reminded me of something from an old movie or place envisioned reading a book. We loved travel and adventure, but we also loved our home and our country. We drove the car straight to the airport where we caught the plane for home. It had been a great and wonderful trip.

But even with the sense of welcome from generations past, in the winds and the waves, my sense of place is in America. My ancestors crossed the vast ocean centuries ago to make their home and to make it what it is today so that generations could be born and live here without the struggles and sacrifices they endured. They spoke in the wind and waves, and they left an imprint on this land that is still burning like a candle with an endless wick. They are still ready to tell their stories and share the lives they led with their descendants, if only we will stop and take the time to

listen at the ocean's edge.

www.ingramcontent.com/pod-product-compliance
Lightning Source LLC
Chambersburg PA
CBHW030641260626
47157CB00007B/2427